Love on the Brain

By
Natavia

SOUL Publications

"A great soul serves everyone all the time. A great soul never dies. It brings us together again and again." ~ Maya Angelou

Kyst
The Lab

Friday, December 13th 2019

My heart dropped to the pit of my stomach as the judge gave me a double life sentence for killing a cop who tried to kill me. My lawyer suggested a plea deal but fuck that, it was kill or be killed. The family of Officer Daniels cheered for getting the justice they felt they deserved while my family cried out for me. I held my head up and didn't show any remorse for what I did. Officer Daniels had been harassing me for two years and even broke my nose, but did I get any justice? Fuck no! The racist asshole still had his job after all the reports I filed against him. I was an honor-roll student and had an athletic scholarship but it was all taken away because Officer Daniels pulled me over on an illegal stop.

"What would you like to say to the family of Officer Daniels?" the white male judge asked while the all-white jury looked at me with hate-filled eyes.

"If I could do it again, I would. Fuck that muthafucka!" I shouted and the court room was in an uproar. What did they expect me to say, that I regretted it? He was one less racist officer off the street, is how I saw it. I was done feeling sorry for myself. I had been a target of the system that was supposed to be equal for all. They didn't care that I worked my ass off so that I could play pro football and to get my mother out of poverty. They didn't care about any of it because they looked at Officer Daniels as a hero for risking his life while stopping me from committing a crime before I even committed one. So, not only was I a cop killer, apparently I was a gang member of a drug organization, too. All of which was a lie.

"I love you, Kyst! I'm so sorry!" my mother cried. I was escorted out of the court room through a side door.

"You are stuck with us now," a black officer named Brown said to me.

"Fuck you, too!" I spat.

"You think you're tough, huh? You know what they do to niggas like you?" he asked. Correctional Officer Brown hated my guts and one time when him and another C.O. escorted me to a hearing, I ended up in the infirmary.

I kept quiet to make sure the ride back to the prison was a bearable one. A van was waiting for me behind the courthouse because the streets were filled with protestors. The city of Annapolis hadn't been the same in two months, which is how long it took them to sentence me while the cops who murdered innocent civilians never even made it to trial. The law couldn't wait to have me rot in jail. The officers pushed me into the door of the van, busting my lip. I was very weak and could barely stand on most days because I was starving. Whenever I did eat, it was just enough to keep me alive because I was iffy about the prison guards poisoning me. My mother put money on my books plenty of times, but it somehow disappeared. I couldn't understand why the world hated me because of a man like Officer Daniels.

The inside of the transport van was like a cage, the kind they use to pick up stray animals. My lip was bleeding, seeping through my orange jumpsuit from my face being slammed into the van's door. My father was looking out for me because, after all the trauma I had to my face, I still had all of my teeth.

"That animal won't last long in general population," Officer Brown said to the officer who was driving.

"That's if he makes it there," the officer replied.

"Where are y'all taking me?" I asked when the van went in the opposite direction of the prison.

"Shut up back there! You belong to us now!" the driver said. "He might die anyway," he added, purposely going over a pothole. I wasn't buckled down in the seat, so my neck jerked, almost snapping from the impact. My body was uncomfortable lying between the seat and the barrier that separated me from the officers. Luckily, I was able to pull myself back up on the seat.

We drove about two hours from the city until we stopped at a gate in a deserted town called Rockstone. It had been abandoned because of a flood that ripped through the small town, killing many of its people eighty years ago. I checked out my surroundings and there were military vehicles and men in uniform in the area. The driver of the van spoke to a man in uniform at the gate in a different language. Seconds later, the gate opened to what looked like an old hospital. I had a bad feeling that something dangerous was lurking ahead.

"Get out of the van!" Officer Brown said after he opened the door.

"Get off of me! I can walk, muthafucka!" I said when he snatched me out.

He took his stick, jabbing me in the stomach with it, causing me to double over. I almost threw up, but my stomach was empty. Four military men, along with Officer Brown and the driver of the van, escorted me inside the hospital. There was a rancid smell that was enough to knock someone out. Blood decorated the halls and walls and dead rats were scattered across the floor. The hospital was too quiet with only the sounds of my shackles clanking with each painful step I took.

Love On The Brain   Natavia

Officer Brown pushed me through a double door to a cleaner hallway that was freezing cold like the morgue. Old hospital stretchers were aligned against the walls. We came to another double door at the end of the hall. One of the men in uniform pressed a button on the wall and a man's voice came through an intercom asking for a code. A man responded into the intercom in a foreign language and the doors immediately opened.

Maybe this is a new prison for people who have to serve a life sentence.

This hallway was different than the other two. There were people in display rooms the size of a closet. There was no way in hell I was spending my life in a small space like that. I'd rather die trying to escape. A black man with shackles around his ankles threw his body against the plastic window. It felt like I was in a haunted house as I stared at him. The man's pupils were cloudy white as a dark green liquid goo dripped from his mouth. His skin was the color of gray mold on bread with infected sores covering his body.

"This isn't a prison! This has got to be hell!" I said as I was pushed further down the walkway.

Boom!

A woman was banging her head against the window of her cell and her eyes were the same as the man's who was throwing his body against the window. The only difference between the two of them was that her body wasn't as decayed as his. I thought they were the only two that way—I was hoping they were—but I counted many more as we walked further down.

"You'll be like them next," Officer Brown said.

"You helped bring all these people here? There are only black people in those rooms! You're a fucking sell out!" I said to Officer Brown.

"You think I care about those criminals? Nobody will miss them! My people, huh? My people didn't give a fuck about me. I was poor and bullied because I didn't have the newest pair of Jordans! My fucking people tormented me all throughout high school, especially the jocks like you who made my life miserable. I bet you never had that problem. See, when you're poor but can play sports, not wearing name brand shit doesn't matter. You'll never understand how my people treated me but now I hold the power, Kyst. I control you," Officer Brown said to me.

"You can't control shit if you're being controlled. If this thing blows up, they're going to blame you for it all. The system doesn't work for you either and it won't work unless we stick together."

The other officers laughed at me and Officer Brown joined them. I continued walking, but the shackles around my ankles were beginning to cramp my legs. Officer Brown pushed me when I slowed down. The doors at the end of the never-ending hallway opened.

I hope this is the last hallway.

Two white men and an Asian man came out of the doors wearing lab coats. The white man who looked to be in his late fifties to early sixties took a chart from Officer Brown.

The man with the chart must be in charge. All of these bastards are sick!

"He's that popular kid that's always on the news. Wow, what a waste in talent. Let's see, he's six feet-one and weighs one-hundred and eighty pounds. He looks a little smaller than that," the one reading my chart said.

"What are you doing to these people? Are you turning them into lab rats? Why is it only people that look like me in those cages?"

"Be careful with this one. He thinks he's Fred Hampton," Officer Brown said sarcastically.

"His blood is rare, AB-negative. This vaccine might not work," the man said. The Asian scientist took the chart, scanning through it.

"This is perfect! With his rare blood, maybe the vaccine will respond differently to his red blood cells," the Asian man said.

"GET OFF ME!" I shouted when I was dragged into an operating room. The table in the middle of the room had chains and thick leather straps for restraint. Officer Brown punched me in the chest as I fought to get out of their grasp.

"You're going to make it worse, kid," Officer Brown said when he punched me again. After the crucial blow that almost knocked me out, the scientist strapped me down to the table. From the corner of my eye, I saw one of the men in a lab coat give Officer Brown an envelope. He opened it, pulling out stacks of money.

"I guess I can get those J's I always wanted," Officer Brown said. He slapped the money across my face.

"They are going to find us!" I told him.

"You all are state property, you think the government cares about missing rapists, drug dealers, thugs and cop killers? The world will be a better place without you ghetto trash. I'll see you when you wake up looking like those monsters out there," Officer Brown said to me. He and the military men left the room, leaving me with the three men in lab coats.

I'm dreaming. This can't be it for me. Wake up, Kyst!

The Asian man grabbed a tray full of tubes filled with a green dark liquid. On the tubes was the word, *F-virus.*

"My name is Dr. Richmond, and these are my colleagues, Dr. Wang and Dr. Scott. We're here to help you. As you know, the flu kills more African Americans than any other race due to underlying health issues, plus many can't afford healthcare. With this new vaccine, we can save a lot of you. I promise we're not here to hurt you," Dr. Richmond said.

"I know you saw my IQ score in my chart, therefore you've got to be one dumb piece of shit if you think I believe you. If I wake up from this, I'm going to kill each and every one of you! I'm going to kill you all!" I shouted. Dr. Richmond injected the dark green liquid into my arm.

"ARGGHHHHHHHHHHHHH!" I shouted as my heart raced. My body was burning like someone threw gasoline on me and lit a match. I choked on the blood that came out of my mouth. They were setting the inside of my body on fire. I shook uncontrollably.

"He's not going to make it. He's going to turn like the rest," Dr. Richmond said. What did I do to deserve this? My life flashed before my eyes as I flatlined...

Kyst
Officer Daniels

Two months ago...

*T*he streets were crowded as the protestors were marching for a young man who was slain by a police officer. I looked at the meter and it was almost sixty bucks because of the traffic. The capital of Maryland, Annapolis, was a very small city therefore it didn't take much to jam up the city. I lived on campus at my college which was close to an hour away from my mother's house and every other weekend I came home to visit my family.

"Aye man, you can let me off right here."

"Are you sure? These crowds can get a little wild," the cab driver said.

"I don't blame them. The police officers have been on some bullshit lately and they're getting away with it."

"You just be careful," he said, pulling up to a corner store.

I gave him sixty-five dollars before getting out of his cab. The walk to my mother's house wasn't a long one. I took a shortcut, cutting through a pissy alley. I had to rush so I wouldn't make my mother late to work. It was my twentieth birthday and every year my mother made me a cake. I looked at the time on my cellphone, I had a few hours before the party my teammate was having off campus since it was the weekend.

Fifteen minutes later, I walked into my mother's house. It was always good to be home, even if it was just for a couple of hours. My brother Isiah was in the living room playing his PlayStation.

"What's up, bro?" I asked, giving him a fist pound.

"Nothing, cooling. Can I go to the party with you tonight?" he asked. Isiah was eighteen years old. He didn't play sports; he was heavily into music especially playing the piano.

"Hell no, bro, you got to stay here and watch Camren when Ma goes to work tonight."

Camren is our nine-year-old baby sister.

"Aight whatever," he said.

"The next one you can go with me."

"Aight, bro, I'm going to hold you to that," he said.

I went into the kitchen and my mother was at the stove putting icing on the cake she made from scratch. Her cakes were the best; she actually sold them on the side for extra money. I kissed her cheek as I greeted her.

"Happy birthday, honey."

"Thank you, Ma, it smells good in here. Where's Camren? She usually runs to the door when she hears me."

"Next door at Cree's getting her hair done. She should be finished soon. Every time she goes over there, she never likes coming back," she said.

"I'll go get her."

"And don't you be mean to Cree," she said.

"I'm not going to be mean to her."

"You better not, that girl helps me a lot," she said.

I left out of my mother's house, going next door. I checked myself out in the glass of the door to make sure I looked decent. I used to tease her when we were younger because she was different from the rest of the girls in the hood and in school. It wasn't until I got older that I understood Cree's outlook on life when it came to racism. I'd never paid attention to any of that shit, figured I didn't have to since the segregation days were over. It took a broken nose from a police officer to fully understand Cree.

My waves are still fresh.

I knocked on the door. "Come in!" Cree shouted. I opened the door and the smell of fried chicken hit me. My stomach was grumbling, but since I was ready to eat cake, I couldn't have it; Coach was strict on what the football players ate.

I walked into the kitchen and Camren was sitting at the table eating chicken with a greasy face.

"Happy birthday, Kissed," Camren said.

"Stop calling me that, baby girl," I said. I don't know what my mother was thinking naming me Kyst since it was pronounced Kist. Camren had been calling me Kissed since she was a year old and refused to pronounce it right.

"You walked into my house and can't speak to me?" Cree asked, draining the chicken of grease.

"Do you want a kiss or something?" I asked.

"Imagine that," she replied smartly.

I walked over to her, leaned down and kissed her lips.

"I know you didn't just kiss me, Kyst! Get the hell away from me," Cree said, wiping it off. Cree was nineteen years old and extra thick for her age. She had a darker skin tone with kinky hair that she wore out in a wild mane. Nonetheless, she was a gorgeous girl and I'd been chasing her for a while, but she wouldn't give me the time of day.

"I'm telling Mommy that you're being a perverttttt," Camren sang.

"Shut up!" I replied.

Cree punched me on the arm. "Don't talk to my bestie like that," she said. My eyes scanned her ass when she turned around to get the French fries out of the pot. Cree was wearing a pair of gray leggings with a Malcom-X shirt. She was an activist and cared for the community which sometimes drew negative attention her way because of the neighborhood drug dealers. But Cree was built different, she came from a family of Black Panthers. She turned around and I turned my head, pretending that I wasn't staring at her.

"You want to go to the party with me?" I asked her.

"No, I have a paper to do on The Raid of Harpers Ferry," she said. Cree was going to college for African American studies so that she could teach Black History.

"A waste of time."

"Is that why you stood me up when I held a protest for Cashius?" she asked. Cashius was a young boy from our neighborhood killed by a police officer in front of the mall because of a suspected robbery a month prior. I told Cree I was going to help her out with posters to protest, but I stood her up for a girl.

"Let it go, Cree."

"You've become a target of police brutality and the people want to hear your voice. Why aren't you taking it seriously? You out of all people should've been there," she said.

"Officer Daniels was fired which is a start. Why do you want to waste your life on this when history will always repeat itself?"

"You're sounding just like the people you hang with. Officer Daniels might have been fired but we still have to put the pressure on the police department for the other crimes they have committed," she said.

"And we can worry about that later but give yourself a break!"

"I'll never take a break from this, Kyst. This is who I am, and it's not just about the killings. Have you noticed all of the missing persons posters across the city? Why are there so many black men, women and children going missing and nobody is doing anything about it? Just because you play football and might go to the pros doesn't mean your black problems go away. You need to do better and get your ass out there and protest!" Cree said.

"Okay, Cree, I'll do it. I'll show my face at the party for about an hour then I'll come back and help you do whatever," I replied.

"My brother likes you," Camren said, taking her chicken bones to the trash can.

"Ewwww," Cree said.

"That's what I think, too," Camren said.

"Go home, Camren. We're ready to cut the cake in a few," I said.

"Alright, I'll be back, Cree," Camren said. Shestuck her tongue out at me on her way out of the kitchen.

"It's the weekend and you can start your paper tomorrow. Slide through the party with me for an hour."

"I have better things to do. You know I don't like the type of friends you have," she said.

"Because Jacob is white?"

"No, because they overlooked your issue with Officer Daniels. You need friends that understand you; it's not only about color. But anyways, have fun at that party because I know you're not staying for an hour," she said.

"Can you at least think about coming to my game next Saturday?"

"Why are you being nice to me, huh? Every time you come around you want me to go somewhere with you. I'm not even your type," she said.

"You don't know what my type is and it's not that serious."

"I know your type isn't me," she said.

"You got a man or something?"

"I'm dating someone," she said proudly.

That nigga ain't me.

"Whatever yo, I'll be back."

I kissed Cree's lips again then rushed out of her house before she could curse me out.

"Hurry up, Kyst. I have to be at the diner in thirty minutes!" my mother shouted from the kitchen after she heard me come into the house. I walked into the kitchen to see Camren and Isiah standing next to the cake, waiting to sing to me.

"I'm here, I had to make sure I turned the stove off," Cree said, coming inside. She rolled her eyes at me, probably still in her feelings because I kissed her twice.

"Awww shucks. Cree is in the building," Isiah said, elbowing me.

"Cut it out!" I elbowed him back.

"Okay everyone, let's sing Happy Birthday," my mother said. She cut off the light, and as they sang Happy Birthday to me, I thought about my father. He died on my ninth birthday in his sleep. His death was a mystery because he was a healthy man from what I could remember. I prayed that he continued to watch over me as I blew out the candles.

"We have something for you," my mother said, grabbing a small bag from underneath the cabinet. I opened the long box that was inside the bag and it was a necklace with a diamond cross pendant.

"That way you can feel protected when you're away from home," my mother said.

"This is lit! I appreciate this," I said to my family.

"Cree pitched in, too," my mother said.

"Sort of," Cree said with a smirk.

She doesn't hate me after all.

"What did you wish for, bro?" Isiah asked.

"I can't tell y'all that."

"I've got to go and clean up the kitchen before my grandmother gets home. I'll get my piece of cake later," Cree said, leaving out of the kitchen.

"Did you ask her out yet?" my mother asked after Cree left.

"I don't like her like that, but I did ask her to go to the party with me."

"Now you know that girl doesn't party. Do something romantic like taking her to a museum or a movie. She's that type of girl," my mother said.

"Any girl would be happy to go out with me. I'm Kyst Macklin, Ma. I shouldn't have to do all of that."

"You're seriously a jock. My heavens I wasn't expecting that. Anyway, here's my car key. Have fun and do not drink nothing, Kyst, and if you do decide to be grown, catch a cab. I'm trusting you with our transportation," she said.

I thanked her, excited that she trusted me with her car. Since I was a full-time student and didn't have a job, I couldn't afford a vehicle. My mother was already working extra hours to buy me clothes and shoes so asking for money for my own car would've been selfish of me.

"Stephanie is here to take me to work. Be safe and don't be too grown," my mother said, giving me the side-eye.

"I'm not messing with girls tonight. I'm just hanging with the fellas."

"Ummm hmm," she said, grabbing her purse and jacket off the kitchen chair. She wished me Happy Birthday one more time before leaving the house. Isiah and Camren could eat a whole cake by themselves, so I cut a piece for Cree and wrapped it up, storing it in the fridge. My cellphone rang and it was my homeboy Jacob calling me.

"Come on, bro. We started the party early," he said after I answered the phone. I had a mouth full of cake.

"I'll be there."

"Melody is asking for you," he said.

"I hate that bitch. If she's there I'm not coming."

"I'll tell her to leave," Jacob said.

"Who invited her anyway?"

"I did, I thought you two were back talking again," he said.

"Why in the fuck would I talk back to her if I don't like her?"

"Bro, she told me you two squashed the beef and it was a big misunderstanding. I'll tell her to leave right now. Hurry up," Jacob said. Jacob was a white boy, but he acted like a brother. We'd been close since freshman year of college. His family was like my family and vice versa. Melody was a white girl, too. I had sex with her one time and somehow her father found out. I wasn't the only black man his daughter had been with but for some reason, me and her talking struck a nerve. That's what Cree meant when she said she wasn't my type. Melody was the only white girl I got involved with out of my twenty years of life and I deeply regretted it because of what her father had put me through.

"Lock up and y'all don't touch Cree's cake. I wrapped it up and put it in the fridge for her. That's y'all asses if someone eats it."

"I gotcha, bruh," Isiah said while he played on the game. Camren was sitting on the couch playing with her Barbies. I told them I was going to see them in a few as I was leaving out. I got into the driver's seat of my mother's 2010 Malibu, starting up the engine.

While I was at a red light, I was listening to Travis Scott's song "Sicko Mode." I couldn't wait to party with my homeboys from school. Jacob sent me a text telling me that Melody left. The light turned green and I pulled off. I was barely out of my neighborhood when a cop told me to pull over through a speaker on his car.

"Damn it! Not on my birthday. My mother is going to be hot!" I said to myself. I hurriedly grabbed my license and the registration and sat them on the dashboard. My heart was beating out of my chest when I realized it was a white cop. All cops weren't bad but not all cops were good. It was nine o'clock at night and dark out. I didn't have a clear view of his face as he got closer to the driver's side window.

"Step out of the car, Kyst," the familiar voice said. I squinted my eyes, putting my arm over my face to shield them from his flashlight to make sure I wasn't tripping. My mother complained to the Towson police department numerous times because Officer Daniels had been harassing me since I was eighteen. It had been two years since I slept with his daughter.

"You were fired, and you still haven't learned your lesson," I said.

"I got transferred to a different precinct. Looks like I'm going to be in your neighborhood a lot," he said.

"Why am I being pulled over?"

"Where's your manners, boy? When you address me, it's Sir!" he said.

"I have a restraining order against you! I don't have to do shit!" Officer Daniels chuckled as if he knew something I didn't.

"I'm the law, Kyst, and those rules don't apply to men like me. Now, all you have to do is sit still while I run the tags. Matter of fact, I think this vehicle was reported stolen," he said.

"Bullshit! It's in my mother's name!" I said.

"Well then you don't have anything to worry about," he said. He went to the back of my mother's car, calling in her tag number through his walkie-talkie. I knew my rights and what he was doing was illegal, but Officer Daniels was right—the law was meant for men like him. He wasn't supposed to have a job for what he did to me. For two years, he stalked me, making my life hell. Suddenly, I heard glass being shattered. I looked in the rearview mirror and saw him smashing out my mother's tail lights. He desperately needed a reason to pull me over.

"Yo, what the fuck did you do that for? I haven't talked to your daughter in two years!" I said to him.

"Step out of the car with your hands up now!" he said.

"This is some bullshit!" I said. I reached for my phone to record the situation since he was framing me and just in case he shot me.

"Get your black ass out of the car, boy!" he said with his gun pointed at me. I pulled away from my cellphone in the cup holder in fear that he'd shoot me for reaching for what he thought was a weapon. Whatever I did, I had to play it safe to make it out of this alive. I got out of my mother's car with my hands up. Tears stung the brims of my eyes because I knew this wasn't going to end until one of us was dead. As far as I was concerned, the real criminal was Officer Daniels.

"It ain't fair how you muthafuckas start shit for no reason," I said, when he patted me down.

"You got drugs on you?" he asked.

"Fuck no!"

Cars were stopping in the middle of the road and the people at the gas station had their phones out, possibly recording what was going down. I felt a sense of relief since I had witnesses. Officer Daniels dropped a bag of cocaine by my feet on the sly when he patted me down by the ankles.

"Looks like your football career is over," he said. He picked the nickel bag of white powder up, waving it in my face.

"You're busted, buddy!" he said.

"That ain't mine! You're framing me!"

"I know you're going to that party where my daughter is, and you've got another thing coming if you think you're going to be dealing cocaine there. You are under arrest!" he said, slamming me against the car.

"Let him go!" someone yelled out.

"Get the fuck off of me!" I said, when he put his arms around my neck. Officer Daniels was taller than me by an inch and probably weighed close to two-hundred and seventy pounds. He was a big man compared to my one-hundred and eighty pounds. He wrestled me to the ground, yelling for me to stop resisting while calling for back up.

"Get off of him!" the crowd said, now surrounding my mother's car. I wasn't going to die; I couldn't let him gain another victory by taking my life. I'd seen the outcome many times with police and unarmed black men. I couldn't go out like that. I bit his arm as hard as I could. A few onlookers were telling me to stop resisting but if I stopped, he would kill me. I was trying to get away and I managed to crawl onto the sidewalk. Officer Daniels rushed me, striking me on the arm with his baton. He sat on my stomach then strangled me. His weight was pressing me down onto the cement, painfully scraping my back as I fought to breathe.

"Let him go! You're going to kill him! He's just a kid!" a woman screamed. Officer Daniels had spit foaming in the corners of his mouth while he angrily called me racial names. Despite his animal behavior and him trying to kill me, he was calling me ghetto trash and a thug. I reached for his gun with the little strength I had left.

"He's going to kill him!" someone shouted.

Pop! Pop! Pop! Pop!

I shot him four times, once in the head. His heavy body fell beside me. Officer Daniels' blood ran through the cracks of the sidewalk as I still struggled to catch my breath. I got on my knees with my hands behind my head when a squad of police cars pulled up to the scene. The greatest thing of all, I wasn't physically dead, but I knew they were going to spiritually kill me anyway.

Cree

The Detective

December 19th, 2019 (Present Day)

*I*t's been six days since Kyst was sentenced to life in prison. The city was in an uproar because of the riots and protesting. We all knew Kyst was innocent and acted in self-defense. What else was there to do since Officer Daniels got away with harassing him?

I slowly climbed out of bed because my grandmother was downstairs cooking breakfast. I'd spent many days in my bedroom, crying my eyes out because I couldn't protect Kyst. He used to be an asshole to me, since we were in elementary school, but he wasn't the thug they painted him out to be. My grandmother was putting a stack of pancakes on a plate when I went to the kitchen table.

"Good morning, baby," she said.

"Good morning, Nanny."

"You were up crying over Kyst again I see. Your eyes are swollen," she said.

"It's not fair that he sits behind bars for the rest of his life. I should've gone with him to that party when he asked. Maybe Officer Daniels wouldn't have pulled him over if he saw that Kyst wasn't alone. This is my fault."

"You have to stop it, Cree. You can't keep doing this to yourself," she said.

"Didn't you see him at the trial? He lost weight and there was so much sadness in his eyes. His soul was taken away from him. That judge was biased! He had proof that Officer Daniels harassed Kyst for two years and didn't do anything! This world isn't fair, Nanny. If they aren't killing us, they are putting us away like animals."

"He shot a cop, Cree, with his own weapon. You know they don't care about anything else," she said.

"A cop that wasn't supposed to be a cop. That's the fight, Nanny, we need to hold the police department accountable for hiring him. I won't rest until we do."

"I'm sixty-three years old, baby. I cannot worry about you risking your life for Kyst. This city is in an uproar and the police are extra trigger happy with the riots and protests. Let it go until everything dies down," she said.

I moved to Annapolis, Maryland with my grandmother when I was nine. My parents died in a car accident because a white man drunk driving ran into them after running a red light in Texas. Now I was reliving that moment again because I lost someone important to my life again. My grandmother handed me a tissue as tears fell down my face.

"You're a strong girl, Cree. You'll get through this," my grandmother said.

"This is a cycle, Nanny. It's like a genocide going on in front of our eyes."

"What do you want to do? Go out there and kill people?" she asked.

"YES! It's a war and I'm tired of sitting on my ass."

"Watch your damn mouth in my house! Enough is enough! This is a battle that you cannot win, baby, not now anyway. Besides, we will be getting our reparations soon, that's justice enough. At least a lot of families won't have to struggle anymore," she said.

"I don't care about that. I don't believe we will be getting that money, anyway, trust me. They'll find a way to stop it, maybe that's why people are going missing now."

"My heart breaks for my people but sacrifices have to be made in order to survive this world. Are you having those dreams again?" Nanny asked.

"No. Beth has been quiet for some years now."

"I hope she stays quiet. You're getting too old for imaginary friends," Nanny said.

"She'll come back," I joked, getting under my grandmother's skin.

"Yeah yeah," she chuckled.

I had blueberry pancakes, bacon, grits and eggs on my plate with a glass of fresh squeezed orange juice to wash the food down. Seeing Kyst's frail body made me not want to eat. How dare I have that luxury of eating a fresh home cooked meal while he starved. Maybe I was being hard on myself, but I should've gone with him. I took my plate upstairs as my grandmother cleaned the kitchen. There was a picture of me and Kyst in my room next to my bed. We were in high school when his mother took the picture of us. Kyst had his arm around my shoulder and I faked like I was mad, but I actually had butterflies because of his closeness. Kyst was extremely good-looking with an arrogant, but boisterous attitude. His skin was the color of sand and he had pretty honey-colored eyes. He had a few freckles on the bridge of his nose that added to his uniqueness.

I got comfortable on my bed before I turned on the local news. A Latina reporter was live in front of a hospital in Baltimore, speaking on the increase of flu-related deaths. Not once did she mention the missing men, women and children. It seemed like nobody cared about them.

I changed the channel, going to my Netflix app to catch up on episodes of *The Last O.G.* As soon as I got comfortable, there was a commotion going on outside. I looked out of my window and Kyst's mother, Natalie, was crying as Isiah held her up from falling out onto the lawn. I hurriedly put on a pair of pants, along with slippers before storming out of the house.

"What happened? Is everything alright?" I asked Isiah. He, too, was sobbing.

"My baby is dead," Natalie said.

"WHAT!" I screamed.

"He died from the flu. Apparently, a lot of inmates had it," Natalie said.

"I'm sorry, ma'am," the detective said.

I could tell by his body language that he didn't care. His hands were in his pockets as he annoyingly looked around. He was probably ecstatic that Kyst was dead.

SOUL Publications

"Kyst was murdered! Just be honest and tell the truth! We saw the bruises on his face at trial!" I screamed. I charged towards him, but someone was holding me back. That person was my grandmother.

"You can come down to the morgue to identify him after his body is transported. Again, I'm sorry, ma'am. You all be safe," the detective said to Natalie.

"They killed him. He was probably beaten to death. Kyst would've told somebody that he was sick. I don't believe it."

"Now is not the time, Cree," my grandmother said.

"I can't take this. I won't accept it. We've been getting death threats, I lost my job, my car and I can barely afford to keep our home and now my son is dead. My baby is gone," Natalie sobbed. I hugged Isiah, rubbing his back as he cried on my shoulder. Kyst's family was suffering—we all were suffering. I couldn't remember the last time I went to my classes at the community college. My grandmother helped Natalie into her house with me and Isiah in tow. Natalie's home used to be neat and tidy, but now it was junky. I tried numerous times to help Natalie around the house and with Camren, but she refused it. The whole situation completely broke my heart. Isiah was a wreck, too; he was no longer going to school because he was also getting death threats. The system left Kyst's family out to die and nobody seemed to care about them but me.

"Excuse me for my house," Natalie said. She knocked two pizza boxes off the couch before she sat. Isiah went upstairs, slamming his bedroom door.

"I know Kyst was murdered. I can feel it. My baby died alone in that filthy prison," Natalie said.

"Or he really could have had the flu. I heard from a lady down at my church that her grandson also died from a flu in prison," my grandmother said.

"What race was he?" I asked with sarcasm.

"He was African-American," she responded.

"If that's the case, Kyst would've told me he was sick," Natalie said.

"Maybe he didn't want to tell you so you wouldn't panic," my grandmother replied. She was pissing me off, pretending that Kyst died from the flu. I understood what she was trying to do; my grandmother wanted to defuse the situation, but we didn't have time for those games. We had to acknowledge the mystery of Kyst's death.

The tears were still coming down Natalie's youthful face as my grandmother consoled her. Natalie was forty years old, but she looked much younger. She could pass as Kyst's older sister. She had the same skin tone and hazel eyes as him. Kyst had a lot of his mother's features.

"Kyst was murdered and we need to hire our own medical examiner," I said. I quickly wiped the tears from my eyes, on the verge of bursting into tears.

Hold it together Cree. Do not break down yet, you have to be strong for Natalie.

"I don't have the money for that. I'm burnt out from spending what I had left on Kyst's lawyer. We're so broke that we might have to move into a shelter," Natalie said.

"Can your church raise money for Natalie's family?" I asked my grandmother and she cut her eyes at me. I couldn't figure out why she wasn't showing much sympathy for Natalie and her children. My grandmother knew how sick and twisted law enforcement could be, but she was believing the flu rhetoric the detective gave to Natalie.

I got off of Natalie's couch to clean up her living room. The last thing I wanted was for her to be depressed in a filthy house. I was hoping a clean house would give her a little normalcy. Camren came downstairs while I wiped off the coffee table. She was rubbing her eyes as she stood in the middle of the living room. She was still somewhat asleep.

"Why are you crying, Mommy?" Camren asked Natalie, waking completely up.

"I'm fine. I'm just a little sad that Kyst isn't home," Natalie said.

"Me, too. I miss him," Camren said.

I guess it wasn't the right time to tell Camren that Kyst is dead.

"Want to help me clean up the kitchen?" I asked Camren.

"Okay," she said with a smile.

Since Camren was the only girl, I took on the role of her big sister. When I wasn't busy with school and my part-time job at Chipotle, I used to take her to the mall. I felt guilty again for spending my time locked up in my bedroom instead of getting Camren out of the house.

"Are you sad, too?" Camren asked as I ran the sink water.

"Yes, I miss Kyst."

"He had a crush on you," Camren said.

"I had one on him too. I should've told him while he was here that I liked him."

"Write him and tell him. I'm going to write him later," she said with a smile on her face.

"I will."

"We have to do it soon because I'm going with my father later on," she said. Camren was a cute little girl with thick coily hair and high cheekbones. She was also dark brown, the same as me. Camren had a different father than her brothers. Kyst's mother got pregnant a few years after her husband died.

An hour later, someone knocked on Natalie's door while I was moping the kitchen floor.

"I'll get it!" I shouted, heading to the door.

My grandmother and Natalie were sitting on the couch drinking tea when I walked past them.

I hope it's another detective to tell us they made a mistake and Kyst is still alive.

I opened the door and it was two of Kyst's friends from Morgan State University. Jacob and Tray were staring down at me with scowls on their faces. I strongly disliked them and vice versa.

"What are y'all doing here?"

"We're here to talk to Natalie. Are you going to invite us in?" Jacob asked. I stepped to the side to let them in. Jacob was the white boy that only had black friends. He was wearing a pair of Timbs, jeans and a black bomber jacket. Jacob wasn't bad looking either, he reminded me of Freddie Prinze Jr. in his younger days. The only difference was that he had blond hair and ice blue eyes. Tray was cute, too, but he was a straight-up asshole though. He put me in the mind of Cookie's youngest son on that show *Empire*.

I told Camren to go upstairs to her bedroom while the adults talked. Natalie waited until she heard Camren's door close upstairs.

"Kyst is dead," Natalie told his friends.

Jacob flopped down on the couch, but Tray wasn't having it.

"They killed him, didn't they? Kyst looked pretty fucked up at the trial. I knew they were doing shit to him, but he denied it whenever I visited him. Damn it! I told you, Jacob! I told you not to invite Melody to that fucking party and now look! Our homie is dead!" Tray said, yelling at Jacob.

"I didn't know how bad it was between those two! Kyst didn't tell us anything about Officer Daniels harassing him!" Jacob yelled at Tray.

"Calm down, everyone! I understand we're all upset but it's not the time to blame each other!" my grandmother spoke up.

"Kyst was a good dude and I know he was going through hell. He wasn't built for none of that jail shit," Tray said.

"He died from the flu," my grandmother said.

"I heard about the flu being bad this year, but I don't believe he died from that," Jacob said. I passed him a tissue as he sobbed. Maybe I judged Kyst's friends because I thought they knew what was going on between him and Officer Daniels and didn't have his back. I went back into the kitchen to finish the floors. The home was much easier to breathe in since me and Camren cleaned up. After I was finished, I went back into the living room and Natalie, Tray and Jacob's cries were getting to me. I hugged Natalie and told her I was coming right back.

"Thank you for everything, Cree. Kyst is very lucky to have had you in his life," she said, squeezing me tightly.

"I'm lucky, too."

I rushed out of the house because I felt myself on the verge of breaking down again. Everything seemed to be a dream. A crackhead riding down the street on a bicycle and the two birds fighting over an old hamburger bun in the middle of the road all seemed to have been in slow motion. My legs were feeling heavy as if I was walking through mud on my way home. Even though I lived next door to Natalie, it felt like I lived three houses down. Once I made it inside the house, I broke down in tears, sliding onto the floor. I called out Kyst's name, praying that it wasn't true, and begging him to come back. Had I known that I was in love with him while he was still alive, I never would've rejected him.

Kyst
Monster

Midnight...

I heard voices as my body rested. For a long time, I thought I could've been dreaming but I knew that I really wasn't. Last, I remember I was being kidnapped by Officer Brown and brought to an old hospital so they could experiment on me. I also remembered when my heart stopped, and everything went dark, so how was I still awake?

Why can't I open my eyes! Wake up!

I heard bloodcurdling screams echoing inside my head followed by shattering glass.

"Get back! Get back!" a man cried. His voice was familiar. He sounded like one of the doctors that injected me with the F-virus.

"STOP! No, let me go!" the man screamed. The smell of fresh blood made my stomach growl, reminding me that I hadn't eaten in days. Suddenly, I smelled smoke followed by more screams. The noise was loud inside my head, wrecking my brain.

Is the place on fire? What is happening? I need to wake up!

"We have to get out of here! Those things are eating people!" someone shouted. My head was throbbing from the sensitivity of my ears. I smelled blood again, but this time it was potent. My eyes finally opened from the sharp hunger pains that ached my stomach.

What in the fuck am I doing in this?

I was inside of a small space, laying on my back. It took me a few minutes to realize I was in a mortuary fridge.

How is this possible? I know I died. Did I come back from the dead?

I kicked at the door, leaving a dent.

Where did my strength come from? I could barely stand at one point.

The door flew open when I kicked it again. I turned on my stomach to crawl out of the freezer. The morgue was old with a harsh smell of mildew, and the walls were falling apart, some cracks I could see through.

This has got to be the old hospital they brought me to.

I was completely naked, but I noticed my six pack. Whatever they did to me, gave me back my old athletic body. I grabbed the sheet out of the freezer I was lying in and wrapped it around my waist.

"Shit!"

I scraped my foot on the uneven cracks in the tiled floor. My blood was the same color as the people I saw in the experiment rooms when I was brought to the hospital. Whatever I was, I was one of them—I was infected. I looked at my hands to see if my complexion was the color of gray mold, but it wasn't. The wound underneath my foot was tightening up. I could feel my skin pulling. When I looked at my foot, the deep cut was healing.

What did they do to me? They turned me into a monster!

An alarm was ringing in my ears as smoke crept into the morgue—it was a fire alarm. I turned the scolding hot doorknob to exit and it burned my hand. There was something on the other side blocking me in. I shoved at the door as hard as I could with my shoulder, pushing away whatever was blocking it. There was a child in the hallway eating the flesh off a man's face. The little girl looked like she was my little sister Camren's age. Sores covered her face as gooey dark green blood dripped from her nose.

"Helllpppp me," the man said when I crept past him being eaten alive. My brother Isiah played games where infected humans ate other humans—they were called Zombies.

Am I a zombie? Is that why the smell of blood woke me up?

The little girl smelled like rusted metal mixed with a rotten carcass. She looked up when she heard me bump into the wall. Her cloudy pupils indicated there wasn't a soul left inside her body. She sniffed the air, reminding me of a predator scoping out its next meal. She went back to eating, chewing through the bone of the man's face.

Maybe she can sense that I'm one of them.

I wasn't a scientist but judging the zombie's reactions, she was possibly blind. Smoke was piling up in the hallway. I rushed through a door that had the name *Boiler Room* written across it.

Boiler rooms are in the basement. If the building is on fire above, the only escape would be down here.

I paused when I saw black people in cages like rabbits.

Warm flesh.

My stomach growled again as my mouth watered from hearing beating hearts pounding inside my head. This is what the scientists wanted; they were doing a genocide, but their plan backfired. Instead, the F-virus had turned us into dead flesh-eating humans.

"Help us!" a woman cried out.

"We can smell the smoke coming down here! Get us out before we burn!" a man shouted.

"That's the kid who killed that cop!" another said.

"I cannot save y'all! There are monsters in this building. You're dead either way," I shouted.

"I'm pregnant!" a woman cried.

There were six cages made out of barb wire with an electricity line at the top. If they touched the fence, it'd shock all of them. Also, if the fire reached the boiler room, they'd die painfully, roasting to a crisp from the electricity.

"Kyst," someone called out.

A young man that looked to be my age was wearing a shirt that read, *Kyst is innocent.*

"You look familiar," I said to him.

"I'm Kejuan. I go to school with Cree. You might've seen me at her house a few times with the rest of us," he said, looking back. I remembered them; they were a part of Cree's organization which was against police brutality.

"When did you get here?" I asked him.

"I came here the same day you were sentenced. We were locked up for protesting. Instead of them taking us to the police station, we were brought here," he said.

Ba-boomp... Ba-boomp... Ba-boomp.

The sound of his beating heart was making my stomach ache badly—I was craving meat. I had to eat but I couldn't wrap my head around eating a human.

"Yo, man, are you alright? Your eyes are changing. They were silver and now they're back to normal. What is this place?" he asked.

"It's a science lab. They are injecting us with a virus to see how effective it is. They are creating a silent killer, passing it off as a flu shot," I told everyone. The room was in an uproar, filled with cries and screams.

"I've seen them come down here to get men and women, even children, but they never come back," Kejuan said.

The noises from the zombies were getting closer, followed by gunshots. Since the zombies were already dead, getting through the electric barriers was going to be a piece of cake.

"If you destroy the electricity line, we can get out," Kejuan said.

I could eat one of them. Just one to satisfy my hunger. No, what am I thinking? I can't do that. I'd rather die! Damn it, I'm already dead.

"I want my mommy," a little girl said with a tearstained face.

The power line that was connected to the cages was more than fifteen feet above my head. I had to climb to get up to it but time was running out.

"Back up!" I told Kejuan and the rest of the people.

I rammed my body into the cage four times before it collapsed; my body was numb to the shock waves from the barriers. The power in the boiler room went out—it was pitch black. I caught a whiff of that awful scent of rusted metal and rotten flesh—the zombies were getting closer.

"Everybody do not move! Whatever you do, don't move or make a sound."

There was a loud bang against the door to the boiler room.

This isn't going to work. These people are going to die.

I must've had X-ray vision because I could see only the beating hearts of the warm bodies surrounding me. I was different than the rest of the zombies. I wondered if it was because of my blood. There was another bang at the door followed by a grunt. The zombies sounded like huffing bears. I could hear them sniffing on the other side of the door—there was more than one.

How in the hell are they running through the building? Somebody must've let them out. I have to stop them from coming in.

I opened the boiler room door and there was three of them: two men including the little girl I saw in the hallway. They sniffed the air as I stood in the doorway, using my body to block the humans' scent that was behind me. Gunshots echoed throughout the hallway and the zombies went to the noise. I breathed a sigh of relief.

"I'm going to look for a way out. Do not move!" I told everyone before leaving the boiler room. I rushed down the hallway, following the gunshots. Six military men were opening fire on the zombies until they collapsed.

One of them pointed a gun at me.

"Wait, don't shoot him!" a man dressed in a lab coat said. It was Dr. Richmond.

Maybe the two other doctors became a meal.

"You're alive," he said.

"Let the people go in that boiler room!" I replied.

"This is unbelievable. You came back and you look incredible," he said.

"We have to leave here before we blow up!" a doctor said, coming out of the morgue; the same room I was in just moments ago. I hurriedly grabbed him, and he screamed for help, dropping the stack of files he was carrying.

"We have to kill him!" a man in military gear said.

"NO! This is remarkable. We can make trillions! Maybe we can use his blood to bring back our loved ones or become immune to the virus if bitten," Dr. Richmond said.

"Fuck all of that you're talking! Let the people in the boiler room leave peacefully!" I shouted.

There are more zombies in this building. I can hear them. These men are doomed, everyone is doomed, but maybe a few can get away to tell what happened.

"Please do what he says," the doctor I had in my grasp pleaded.

"Shut up, Scott!" Dr. Richmond said.

Ba-boomp... Ba-boomp... Ba-boomp!

The chubby doctor I had in my grasp was warm and appetizing! The green veins in my arms protruded. I could feel my body changing, turning into a zombie.

"He's one of them!" a man shouted from behind Dr. Richmond.

"He's different than them! Do not shoot!" Dr. Richmond repeated.

"Please help me!" Scott said, begging for his colleagues to help him. I snatched his head back, exposing his fleshy neck. Scott screamed for help when I took a chunk of meat out of his neck, devouring the tangy, bloody but flavorful brawn. A bullet pierced through my shoulder, but immediately the wound healed. More shots rang out as I ate Scott's neck until he was almost decapitated.

"Hold your fire!" Dr. Richmond said.

I dropped Scott's lifeless body onto the floor in a pool of his own blood.

"Your red blood cells are what causes your wounds to heal so quickly. The vaccine gave you super strength. Come with us, kid, and we'll make your life better. If you escape, you'll be the public's enemy. I'll make sure your family is well off," he said.

"You murdered my people, turning them into monsters! There's a little girl lying on the floor dead and you don't give a fuck," I said, as I took a step forward.

"This building is going to explode in less than three minutes. Everyone is already dead. Even if they are alive now, they won't make it. I'm giving you a chance to come with us!" Dr. Richmond said. A man in uniform shot me in the chest with a shot gun. I charged into him, slamming his body into the wall, shattering his back. A piece of the ceiling fell between me and Dr. Richmond.

"I'll see you again!" Dr. Richmond said before the debris separated us. I undressed the man in uniform that I killed then hurriedly got dressed in his clothes. The building trembled followed by a loud explosion. I grabbed a gun off the floor, along with the files Scott dropped, then rushed towards the boiler room. Kejuan and the rest of the people were in the hallway.

"We have to hurry up, Kyst. We can no longer breathe down here," he said, coughing.

The only way out was to knock down the walls in the morgue since they were weak.

"Come this way," I told them.

I rushed down the other end of the hall, jumping over dead bodies. A piece of the ceiling fell, smashing a few people to the floor.

"Make sure the kids and women go first!" I shouted out.

"This is a dead end," Kejuan said, looking around.

"Take this," I said, giving him the gun.

I tucked the files down in the baggy pants I was wearing.

"The building is falling!" a woman cried out.

I threw myself against the wall, cracking it upon impact. Through the crack, I felt a breeze from outside. I kicked, punched and slammed myself against the wall until I fell through, landing in the woods.

"Hurry up!" I told them, helping them out of the hole. The children went first then women.

"Argghhhhh!" someone yelled.

I peeked through the hole in the wall and a zombie was eating a man. They were coming out of nowhere. I noticed they were falling out of the ceiling into the morgue. Kejuan rushed through the hole, dropping the gun on the ground. Not everyone made it out, but the women and children were safe. Five zombies crawled out of the building before it fell to the ground. I pulled the trigger to shoot one, but the gun didn't have any bullets.

"Fuck!" I shouted. I ran through the woods, yelling for everyone to run faster. The zombies were fast. A zombie woman caught a little girl, tackling her onto the ground. I picked up a rock, smashing the woman's head.

"My ankle!" the little girl cried. I picked her up then took off to catch up with the rest. Gunshots echoed throughout the woods, followed by growls and grunts from the zombies. Once I made it out of the woods, I was in front of a military base, surrounded by tents.

"Surrender now!" a man with a Russian accent said to me with his gun drawn. Out of nowhere, a truck ran him over.

"Get in!" Kejuan shouted out of the window.

I rushed to the black Yukon, as the back door opened, a man held his arms out to take the girl.

"Hurry up! They're coming!" Kejuan said.

I turned around and zombies were coming out of the woods. There were so many of them. Most of them were the military men who were infected. I jumped in the passenger seat, across a woman's lap. Kejuan stepped on the gas as the zombies chased after the truck.

"Go faster!" I shouted.

The woman in the passenger seat climbed to the back to tend to the little girl who was crying in pain.

"Yo, what in the fuck was that back there? People eating people? Those scientists were doing some sick shit!" Kejuan said, almost hitting a tree.

"Watch out!" I said. His hands were jittery as his voice trembled. Everyone was frightened. I was, too, despite being one of them.

"I saw a man get pulled out of this truck and eaten by two people. They shredded him apart. I lost some friends back there," Kejuan said.

"We have to ditch this truck soon. They might have a tracker on it," I said. I was paranoid, worried about Dr. Richmond sending his men to come and find me.

I have to find a way to warn my family.

"Are you one of them?" Kejuan asked.

"If I was one of them, wouldn't I have eaten you already?"

"You broke through a wall, you knocked over an electric fence and walked away from it. A man died in the snap of a finger when he tried to climb the fence. I also noticed those things didn't attack you. I saw your eyes change. Be honest with me because I'm putting their lives in jeopardy with you in here," he said.

"I'm not one of them, but I'm not human either," I replied.

"I guess it's too late for me to have concerns now since I saved your ass back there," he chuckled a little.

"She's running a fever," I heard from the back.

The little girl I saved in the woods was sweating and moaning in pain.

SOUL Publications

"How did they kidnap the children?" I asked Kejuan.

"Foster homes, shelters and juvenile centers, if I'm not mistaken. I heard a few were taken from bible study. This shit is all the way messed up," he said.

A bunch of heartless crooks!

"Another thirty minutes out. We have to ditch this truck."

"Say no more," he replied.

Thirty-five minutes later...

Kejuan stopped near a shopping center. We were less than an hour away from Annapolis.

"I'm out of here. I'm not going back to jail. I've been locked up for five years," a man said before taking off.

"You've got to come with us, Kyst. If they catch you, they'll either kill you or send you back to jail. Nobody will believe us about what happened. They are probably back there cleaning that place up now," a man in a jail suit said to me.

"I'm going to take care of a few things first then I'm out of here."

"Aight man, until we meet again," he said.

He and three others ran off. It was only me, two women, Kejuan and the little girl left.

"We might have to steal a car," a girl said who looked to be my brother Isiah's age.

"Yeah, come on," Kejuan said.

"Who knows how to steal one?" she replied.

"We can figure it out," I chimed in.

"I don't feel too good," the little girl said. Her complexion was changing to a complexion I was all too familiar with. A rash was covering her neck and face and her lips were turning blue—she was dying.

SOUL Publications

"Did you get bit when we were running in the woods?" I asked her. She pulled down her red sweater to show me the bite mark on her shoulder.

"I'm losing my vision, too," she sobbed.

"We have to take her to the hospital," a girl said.

"No, we can't. She's going to turn because she was bitten," I replied.

"We have to make sure she's safe. I can't leave her. We're in the same foster home. She's like a little sister to me," she said.

I hear sirens.

"We've got to dip. We look suspicious with blood all over us," Kejuan said.

"What are y'all's names?" I asked the two women and the little girl.

"I'm Kashawn and this is my foster sister, Armani."

"I'm Gillian. I go to school with Cree and Kejuan," the girl with box braids said.

I looked around, making sure I didn't see anything suspicious. There wasn't a scent of a flesh-eater near which was a good sign. The shopping center was closed, except for a 711 and a twenty-four-hour fitness gym.

"What do you want me to do? Kill her?" Kashawn asked. Dark green blood dripped from Armani's nose after she coughed.

"Screw this. I'll find a way home," Gillian said, walking away.

The sirens are getting closer.

"We have to go!" I said.

"I'll stay right here with her," Kashawn said.

I walked away, looking back at Kashawn and Armani. They were sitting on the sidewalk next to a light pole. I couldn't bring myself to kill a child regardless of what she'd became.

"Psstt!" Kejuan called out to me.

He was hiding behind a Honda Civic when I crept over to him.

"I hear sirens. We need to go now unless you want to be on your own," I told him.

"I don't hear anything. You have special hearing, too?" he asked.

"Yeah, but what are you waiting for?"

"For someone to come out of the gym and rob them," he said.

"We don't have time for that. We will be better off on foot."

"It'll take us two hours to get to the city," he said.

"Muthafucka, I just told you we don't have time. The police will be here in a matter of seconds!"

"Damn it. Let's go. Maybe we can catch up with Gillian," he said.

We ran out of the parking lot, cutting through the woods. Kejuan complained about going back through the woods but it was safe. The flesh-eaters weren't anywhere near. There was a rustle behind a bush along with the sound of sticks breaking underneath a shoe.

"It's a human," I told Kejuan who was hiding behind me. Gillian stood up from the bush, pulling her pants up.

"You two scared the hell out of me!" she said.

"How can you use the bathroom in the woods during a time like this?" Kejuan asked.

"Can we stop fucking around and leave?" I asked the both of them.

"Lead the way, bruh," Kejuan said.

They followed me on the long journey back home. I had a weird feeling it wasn't over, and it was only going to get worse, but I was curious to see how the government was going to spin it around. Dr. Richmond's haunting voice was in my head, telling me that I'd be the public's enemy if I escaped. One thing was for sure though, I had to leave and go someplace very far to hide so that I wouldn't become a slave.

Cree

Wolfsbane

Hours later...

I was laid across the couch in the basement of my grandmother's house, sipping on her old whiskey. Everything was falling apart! Natalie couldn't view Kyst's body due to a very contagious virus and I couldn't get in touch with any of my friends. Maybe it was my fault. I had been distant for the past few months and kept my cellphone off the majority of the time. I called my classmate Gillian for the last time and her phone went straight to voicemail. Gillian was one of my closest friends. I'd met her my first year of college.

"Maybe she's mad at me for ignoring her," I said aloud.

I turned on the news since I was hearing a lot of police sirens in the area. The protestors were still out in the streets even though it was almost

Christmas. The black community was on strike, refusing to spend any money until their voices were heard. I sat up on the couch when I saw a helicopter circling the top of what looked like a burning building.

What in the hell is going on now?

Rockstone was burning to the ground. The town was pretty much historical; it was black-owned until a flood came and wiped it out. I turned the volume up to make sure I heard the news anchor correctly. Rockstone's old hospital was used for prisoners who had to quarantine because of a flu-like virus. A prisoner escaped and somehow set the building on fire.

"This is a state of emergency. Infected prisoners with a rare virus are on the loose," the news anchor said. I called Natalie and she answered on the second ring, her voice cracking up. She was probably crying before I called her.

"Where was Kyst's body at again?" I asked her.

Love On The Brain   Natavia

"They were supposed to transport him to the morgue here. I think they cremated him already. I have been calling around and nobody knows anything," she said.

"I think he was at Rockstone's hospital. They were taking infected prisoners there. The building burned down after prisoners escaped. It's on the news. There is a war going on against our people, Natalie, and we can't sit back and let it continue."

She took a deep breath. "I know that you're going through it, too, Cree, but you're still young and have a full life ahead of you. Your grandmother told me that I should keep you out of my family's business because she doesn't want that burden on you. I have to agree with her so please, going forward, stay out of our business and focus on your future," she said, then hung up on me.

I dropped the phone on the floor in disbelief. How dare my grandmother tell Natalie to not include me? I'd been their neighbor since I moved from Texas. I watched Camren for six years! Maybe I was losing my mind, maybe I wasn't, but I knew the flu had been around for years, so why was it different now? Why were the prisons the only place where this flu so-called existed?

I'm not going to give up on you, Kyst. I'm going to figure out what happened to you. I love you and will always love you.

I took another swig out of the bottle. Just when I was ready to pull out my weed stash, my cellphone rang. My boyfriend, Kejuan was calling me from his house phone. I didn't want to be bothered; how would he feel if he had to listen to me mourn over the man I truly had feelings for. I was ready to turn my phone off, but he called me again.

I'm tripping, it could be an emergency.

"Hello," I groggily answered.

"Cree, come to Kejuan's house now! It's an emergency," Gillian said.

"Oh, thank God I get to hear your voice. I was worried about you."

"Worry enough about me to get here now!" she said, hanging up.

I put a sweater over my bra, stepped into my UGG boots and grabbed my coat, purse and truck key before rushing out the door. My grandmother opened the front door, wearing her house coat.

"Where are you going at three o'clock in the morning?" she asked, after I unlocked the door to my Ford Escape.

"I'm going over Kejuan's."

"Call me soon as get you there," she said.

I waved at her before getting into the driver's seat of my truck. My grandmother closed the door after I backed out of the driveway. I was a little buzzed, but I could see the roads clearly. There was a shot gun that I kept underneath my seat. With all the people that went missing, I had to protect myself from getting kidnapped. I drove through downtown Annapolis which is where Kejuan lived with his roommate. There wasn't anybody outside, not even a police car in sight.

That's odd. I heard so many sirens but haven't seen a cop car yet or any vehicles from the National Guard.

With the roads being clear, I arrived at Kejuan's small townhouse in fifteen minutes. I got out of the truck as soon as I put it in park. My heart was beating out of my chest as I ran up Kejuan's stairs to his front door. I rang the doorbell and Gillian answered it. She looked fine. As a matter of fact, she looked like she was fresh out of the shower and was wearing Kejuan's shirt which came down to her knees.

"Bitch, I know you didn't call me over here to tell me something is going on between you and Kejuan. You could've told me that over the phone! I thought something happened to you," I said, stepping into the foyer.

"I had blood all over my clothes. Come into the living room," she said. Gillian peeked her head out of the door before closing it. I walked into the living room, and someone who resembled Kyst was sitting on a couch facing the entryway of the room. Kejuan was sitting across from the man, facing me.

"What is going on?" I asked Kejuan.

"Don't freak out," he said.

The man with his back facing me stood up. That slow motion feeling happened again as my knees almost gave up on me. I was getting dizzy from holding in my breath as the man turned around to face me. Kyst was standing in front of me, looking better than the last image I had of him in my head. Tears fell from my eyes. He bopped over to me with a smooth stride that only he possessed; he was wearing a military outfit covered in blood.

Maybe I'm really drunk. This has got to be a dream. How did Kyst end up with Kejuan if he's supposed to be dead? Maybe he is dead. Why else would his clothes be covered in blood? I'm losing it! I need to go outside and get some fresh air.

I rushed towards the door, bumping into Gillian on my way out. A pair of strong arms wrapped around my body to keep me from leaving.

"It's me, Cree. Why you acting like you don't see me? I know I'm dead but I ain't a ghost," he whispered in my ear.

My body went crashing to the floor after I fainted from extreme excitement...

Three years ago...

Twelfth grade was the last year of high school. I couldn't wait to leave so I wouldn't have to deal with the assholes. On way way to my locker, after coming out of my third period class, I bump into Kyst.

"Damn, Cree. If you get those eyes fixed, you'll be able to see better," he said. Kyst's friends laughed at his jokes like they always did.

"And if your dick grows two inches, maybe you'll stop acting like a pussy, now move out of my way!" I said, pushing him away from my locker.

Kyst's friends walked away clowning him because I dissed him. He leaned against the lockers as I put in my combination to exchange my books. I had a box of chocolate waiting for me with a cute little teddy bear. Of course, Kyst had to tape a picture of him on the teddy bear; he was so full of himself.

"Happy Valentine's Day," he said, looking down at me with his hazel bedroom eyes. My heart almost skipped a beat when he moved my hair out of my face.

"You have the code to my locker?"

"You've had the same lock since the ninth grade," he said.

"Heyyyyy Kyst," a group of girls sang, walking past. I smacked my teeth when he waved back, showing off his charming smile. They were the "popular crowd" and I was just the "eccentric girl with the wild hair." That's how they referred to me. I was lowkey jealous of the attention Kyst had with the girls which made me push him away.

"You want to go to the movies tonight?" he asked as I closed my locker.

"No, I have to study," I lied.

"I'll study with you then. What class is it for?" he asked.

"No, I'm with a study group."

"Yo, just tell me that you ain't feeling me and I'll back off. Which one of these lames in this school you fuck with?" he asked.

"Which hoe you fuck with, Kyst? Every time I turn around, you are with a different girl. Sorry, I don't want to be a part of your hoe squad."

"Whatever, shorty. I'll be at your truck when school is over so I can catch a ride with you," he said. I blushed when he kissed my forehead. As soon as he walked away, I grabbed the teddy bear out of my locker and held it close to me...

I opened my eyes when a freezing cold hand touched my face. Kyst was staring at me with sparkling silver eyes.

This can't be real. I'm in a twilight zone.

"Finally, you're up," he said.

He was shirtless, and only wearing army fatigue pants. I'd never seen Kyst that buff. *Shit, since it's a dream, I might as well take advantage of it.* He looked at me confusingly when I took my sweater off.

"Shorty, as much as I want to get between those thick thighs, I got to make sure you're okay with me not being the same," he said. I straddled him. "Damn, I didn't know you were this freaky. I would've died a long time ago. I missed your pretty smile while I was away," he said.

I grabbed his face then kissed him, slipping my tongue between his lips. "Make love to me now. These dreams don't last long. I love you so much."

"I love you, too. I always have," he admitted while palming my ass cheeks.

I reached into his pants, grabbing his thick and long dick which was the warmest thing on his body. My pussy throbbed, thinking of how he was going to screw my brains out with his enormous thick veiny dick.

"I thought you was a virgin," he said, side-eyeing me.

"I lost mine in ninth grade."

"With who?" he asked.

"Shut up and take these pants off."

"Are you trying to fuck my woman in my own house?" Kejuan asked Kyst. He punched Kyst on the side of the face. Kyst jumped up and I fell on the floor.

"Woman?" Kyst asked him.

Kejuan looked at me with tears in his eyes. "You're a necrophile! I should've known you wasn't concerned about me. There are no missed calls from you and I've been gone for six days. You probably were out being a hoe!" Kejuan said.

Kyst grabbed him around the neck, slamming him against the wall.

"Put me down!" Kejuan said as he swung his arms.

Dark green veins moved underneath Kyst's skin in a wave pattern.

What is wrong with my man? Is he infected? There is a state of emergency from sick prisoners that escaped but could he be one of them?

Gillian came out of the back room, rubbing her eyes.

"Put him down!" Gillian yelled at Kyst. Kyst made a huffing animal sound as he grunted. He wasn't the jock from next door anymore, he was something else—something dark. His eyes changed, turning into that odd color again. He dropped Kejuan onto the floor and he gasped for air.

I'm seriously seeing weird shit right now.

"I'm not dreaming, am I?" I asked aloud.

"No! I've been trying to tell you that," Kyst said, looking and sounding normal again.

"We were locked in a lab, they were experimenting on us, including Kyst. He saved us—well, some of us didn't make it out alive. It was so horrible, Cree. I saw many of our friends get eaten alive by flesh-eaters," Gillian said, getting emotional. Kyst picked up my sweater and handed it to me.

"Were you all at Rockstone hospital? And what in the hell are flesh-eaters?"

"Yeah, we were there. Are the news reporters talking about it? And flesh-eaters are zombies," Kyst said while looking out of the window.

"Yes, they said a few prisoners escaped with the virus, but screw all of that! Did you say zombies?" I replied.

"Yes, zombies and I'm infected, too, but I don't think it's airborne. A little girl was bitten, and she immediately showed signs. Scientists injected me with a virus that changed me. I'm not human anymore," Kyst said.

"I can't wrap my head around 'zombies.' How is that even possible?" I asked.

"I saw them, too; we all did. They are real," Gillian said.

"Yeah, and your new boyfriend is one of them," Kejuan said as he got off the floor.

"I don't care if you're not the same. I'm going to be with you this time," I said to Kyst, dismissing what he said about zombies. I knew for a fact that zombies weren't real. *Maybe they thought they saw zombies.*

"You mean to tell me, I was out in those streets, protesting for a nigga that you're in love with! You should've told me that you and he had something going on!" Kejuan said.

"I didn't realize it until after he got locked up. At least I told you before me and you got serious."

"Get the fuck out and take Resident Evil with you!" Kejuan replied.

"You're such a lame for this. We're alive because of Kyst," Gillian said to Kejuan.

"My roommate's body was smashed to the ground after that building collapsed. I was in a cage like an animal for six damn days for a woman who is in love with a thug!" Kejuan said. Kyst punched him in his face, knocking him out cold.

"I think you killed him," Gillian said.

"I barely touched him," Kyst replied.

"Your family is worried about you. What are you going to tell them?" I asked Kyst.

"I can't go home. Matter of fact, I only came here so that I can see you one last time. I didn't know that clown was your man though," he said.

"At least say goodbye. You have to put their minds at ease."

"I'm not a human anymore. I'll show you if you don't believe me," he said. Kyst went into the kitchen and came back with a knife seconds later. He cut his arm; a dark green liquid dripped onto the floor. His skin pulled together right afterwards; the wound disappeared like it was never there.

"That's some cool shit. I have to admit," Gillian said.

"I can't go back, Cree. I need a favor from you. Find a way to get clothes and shoes from my room at my mother's crib. I don't want to be around for another minute," Kyst said.

"You're not worried about the flesh-eaters reaching the city and attacking your family? At least figure out a way to stick around since you're not afraid of them," Gillian said to Kyst.

"Them foreign military men probably killed them by now. Trust me, they'll find a way to cover up their tracks. I'm leaving and I'm not going to change my mind," Kyst said.

"I'm going with you. You have to take me with you," I told him.

"Stay here and continue to make sure our community stays safe. I can't let you get involved," he said.

"I'm twenty years old now. I make my own decisions and I'm coming. We can figure out a plan along the way," I replied.

"Let's bounce. I think your lil' boyfriend is about to wake up," Kyst said as Kejuan moved his arm.

Gillian went into Kejuan's roommate's room to grab her pants and shoes. Kyst put on a hoodie, then pulled the hood over his head, shielding his eyes. All three of us left out of Kejuan's house. Kyst sat in the back seat of my truck, ducking down so nobody would see him. My truck was too small for his long legs.

The sun was beginning to peak over the clouds. It was only five days before Christmas, but the holiday spirit no longer existed. My main focus was to make sure Kyst was safe. We were all born for a purpose and my purpose was to protect the man that I loved. I drove through downtown and the road was blocked off. Police cars were everywhere. Kyst was sniffing loudly behind me, sounding like a hound dog. I know he wasn't the same after being experimented on but seeing him go through it was breaking my heart.

"I smell six of them. They made it to the city. I didn't think they'd get this far," Kyst said, sitting up.

"Smell what?" I asked, panicking.

Love On The Brain   Natavia

"I can sense the flesh-eaters. The stronger their scent, the closer they are," Kyst said. Gillian was crying and praying that she wouldn't get eaten. She opened up the passenger door to get out of the moving truck, but I snatched her back.

"Keep still! What is wrong with you?" I yelled at her.

"Bitch, he said they are coming!" she screamed back.

I'm going to play along.

"How close are they?" I asked Kyst.

"Probably ten miles away. Turn off," Kyst said.

I made a sharp turn, going into the opposite direction which was going to make the drive home a longer one. Thankfully, I had a full tank of gas and my shot gun underneath the seat with plenty of shells.

"I have to take my family with me. There's no way I can leave them in this," Kyst said.

Love On The Brain   Natavia

"We can go to Texas; I can talk my grandmother into coming, too. I have an uncle out there," I replied.

"I'm going, too. I'm not staying here after what I saw," Gillian said as she wiped her eyes.

"I'll write down the address," I responded.

"You need to change your name for when you leave this place. You don't want people to call you by your old one," Gillian said to Kyst.

"Wolfsbane is a perfect name," I said.

"The Marvel character?" Gillian asked with her nose frowned.

"No, it's a poisonousness plant. The veins in his skin remind me of one," I replied.

"I'm cool with it," Kyst said.

I was riding past a farm and Kyst told me to pull over so that he could use the bathroom.

"You can't hold it?" I asked.

"I won't be long. I need to go bad, shorty. Pull over behind that tree so nobody sees us," he said. I drove off the road and into the dirt behind a big oak tree. Kyst took off his hoodie before getting out of the truck.

"Are you sure about being with a fugitive? You'll have to make plenty of sacrifices being with someone like him. Your life won't be normal," she said.

"When has our lives ever been normal, Gillian? We are seen as a threat carrying a bag of skittles and an Arizona tea. Our children can't play outside with toy guns without being killed. Our skin in this country will never experience a normal life. Look at what they did to you all at Rockstone. You think that's normal? Life is too short; I'm going to live it to the fullest and experience the love that was meant for us. Kyst being away for two months might not seem like a long time, but I felt like I was dying on the inside. I feel alive again and I won't pass it up."

"Chileeee, you done lost your damn mind but whatever," she said.

"You hoes never see the bigger picture. Love is a force that can't be defeated. Love is what is needed for survival. If our people loved each other more, we wouldn't be the target of America. Love is the weapon to use against the enemy."

"That's the problem, Cree, you are too 'woke.' Sometimes it's okay to pretend these things don't exist. I sleep better that way," Gillian said.

"I'll be sleeping better period because I have Kyst back."

"I'd rather get bitten by a flesh-eater before I give my heart to a man," she said, and I playfully mushed her.

BOOM!

I jumped when a white woman threw herself against my truck, cracking the driver's side window. Dark green liquid dripped from her mouth mixed with red blood. Her eyes were colorless and nasty puss filled sores covered her body—she smelled awful! She pressed her face against the window, spreading her fluids while sniffing us out. She sounded like Kyst when he was sniffing around like a hound dog minutes prior. I screamed as I reached under my seat for my gun, but it was stuck.

"Shoot it!" Gillian yelled.

"It's stuck!" I said.

"There's more!" Gillian panicked. I saw two of them running across the field, heading towards us. Kyst came out of nowhere, tackling them to the ground. I panicked when I didn't have a clear view of him anymore because he disappeared into the tall grass.

"You have to leave him!" Gillian said as the woman banged on my window.

"NO!" I shouted.

I backed my truck up, then pressed on the gas, running the woman over. Half of her body was smashed on the ground, but she was still moving. I saw Kyst running towards the truck in my rearview mirror. I peeled off as soon as he got in the backseat.

"I peed myself," Gillian cried.

I was too shaken up to speak. I couldn't get the image of the woman that ran into my truck out of my head and the rotten stench that was pouring off her body.

"I went a little too far out. By the time I realized they were close by, I hurried back. Some are faster than others. I think the faster ones are newly infected because they aren't as rotten," Kyst said.

"We need to get the fuck out of this city!" Gillian said.

Kyst put his hand on my shoulder. "I'm going to protect you, so you don't have to be afraid when you're with me," he said.

"What about me?" Gillian asked Kyst.

"You're on your own. I just met you," he replied to her. Kyst could be a jackass. I adjusted my mirror and saw that Kyst had blood across his mouth and chest.

"What happened? Are you hurt?" I panicked again.

"I have something to tell you once we get settled," Kyst replied.

I sped towards the direction of our neighborhood, thinking deeply about all the events that had transpired from the moment I walked into Kejuan's house. I remembered Kejuan calling Kyst Resident Evil which is a zombie game. Kyst told me he was infected plus there were changes in his behavior, but he wasn't rotting away nor did he smell dead. He also lied about needing to go to the bathroom because he came back with blood on his body. Maybe he got ahold of a farm animal. I saw his blood when he cut himself and it was dark green, the same as the woman's who I ran over. I wondered how he was different from the rest of the flesh-eaters. I was getting lightheaded as my thoughts wandered, but one thing was for sure; none of it was going to turn me away from him.

Isiah

The Beginning of an Apocalypse

I tossed my brother's football in the air, catching it with one hand. If he was alive, he would've beat my ass if he knew I spent so much time in his room in the basement. Football jerseys from each team he played on since he was eight decorated his wall. I shook my head at the picture of him and Cree sitting on his nightstand next to his bed. They were sitting in front of her grandmother's house wearing Halloween costumes. Kyst was Frankenstein and she was Frankenstein's bride. He denied his feelings for her, but I always knew what it was. I chuckled to myself, imagining the look on his face if I would've teased him with the picture or showed Cree.

I missed by big bro. Even when he went off to college, he still made home feel like home whenever he visited. Now my mother stayed in her room and I stayed in Kyst's room. The doorbell rang, so I went upstairs to see who could be stopping by at six o' clock in the morning. I looked out the peephole and it was that Detective Jamison. He was the man that came by the morning before, giving me and my mother the devastating news about Kyst's death. I opened the door.

"Good morning. Is Natalie home? I want to talk to her about a few things," he said.

"What is it? She's asleep."

"Can I come in?" he asked, peeking around.

"No, you can say what you want to me here."

"With all that's going on, we're trying to make sure the flu doesn't spread for the safety of others. Your brother had friends back at the hospital he was quarantined with and a few of them escaped. Maybe one of them came here," he said, peeking into my house again.

"I don't understand why they'd come here if my brother is dead, or is he even dead? We have no proof, just your word that he died from the flu. There are no autopsy photos, no death certificate, nothing! All I see are a bunch of dirty cops in this area, and I know one when I see one. You're starting to smell dirty, too, bruh."

Detective Jamison didn't have a badge, never showed us one when he stopped by the first time, which led me to believe he knew something about Kyst that we didn't. My mother thought Cree was filling our heads with her crazy theories, but I believed her. Behind Detective Jamison was a black van with a white older man sitting in the passenger seat. It looked like he was wearing a lab coat. I also noticed that Detective Jamison was dressed in military boots and all black clothes. I don't know how I'd almost forgotten the suit he was wearing when I first met him.

"Here's my number. Give me a call if anyone suspicious comes around. These men are infected and need to be quarantined immediately," he said, dropping his card on the ground. I stood in the doorway, watching him get inside the van. In the back seat of the van, I saw a familiar face. It was the black C.O. that escorted Kyst out of the courtroom after his guilty verdict. I closed the front door then rushed upstairs. I pulled down the string that hung from the ceiling, it was a stairway to the attic. Dust got into my eyes; it'd been a year since the attic door was opened. I climbed up the stairs then hit the light switch. A mouse ran across my feet.

"I'm bringing my snake up here for you later!"

I grabbed a pair of binoculars off a crate. There was a small window in the attic I used to spy out of when I was younger. I looked out of the window; the black van Detective Jamison was in was driving up and down the street. An electric company van parked across from my house, but the men inside didn't look like regular workers. I knew military men when I saw them, they had a certain poise to them. The passenger was watching my house.

They aren't even hiding the fact that they're spying on our house. What is really going on?

I saw Jacob walking up the lawn towards our house. Kyst's homeboys were always coming over to check up on us but it was too early in the morning for visitors. He rang the doorbell and I almost tripped going downstairs to get the door. My mother was resting, and I didn't want anyone to wake her up. I opened the door and Jacob stormed into my house.

"Yo, you see what time it is?"

"Yo, some crazy shit is going on. A white dude knocked on my parents' door looking for me this morning and asking questions about Kyst. Luckily, I wasn't home but what is going on?" he asked.

"They are spying on our house and probably your parents' house, too. I don't think Kyst is dead. It seems like they are looking for him but trying to cover it up."

Jacob looked out the living room window. "Bro, this is crazy! On my way here, I saw a man drag a woman out of her car at a red light and bite her. The line was busy when I called 9-1-1 for her. I got to get in touch with Tray to warn him. Maybe they went to his grandmother's house, too," Jacob said. He pulled out his phone to call Tray, but he didn't get an answer.

"I hope he's straight," he said.

"You have a bottle of water? My head is killing me. I partied too hard last night," Jacob said.

"You got white-boy wasted, huh?" I joked as he followed me into the kitchen.

"Always. My parents broke the news to me last night that they are getting a divorce. Yo, can you believe that? A few days before Christmas," he said.

"They probably held on for your sake, but you're an adult now so you all will work it out."

"I don't know how I'll get used to my parents not being under the same roof," he said. I passed him a bottle of water out of the fridge and he thanked me.

"Welcome to the single-parent home club, bruh, but at least you didn't have to grow up like that."

"Ohhh my bad, man. I shouldn't have said anything about that. But can I ask you something?" he asked.

"Go ahead."

"How did your father pass away? Kyst never talked about him, but I've always been curious about it," he said.

"Our father was in the military. I remember him being gone for a year then one day he showed up coughing and spitting up blood. He was in Antarctica and he caught a bad cause of pneumonia. To this this day, I don't understand why he was over there. There's nothing there but scientists and people who study wildlife."

"Sorry about that. I don't know much about the military, but I do know it's very secretive. There's no telling what was going on over there for your father to come back fatally ill," he said.

I wonder why my mother didn't have it investigated.

I picked up the house phone in the kitchen and called Cree to see if they knocked on her door, too. Her phone was off, so I called her grandmother's house. I hated that woman, but she was good friends with my mother.

"Hello," Cree's grandmother answered wide-awake.

"This is Isiah. Did a detective knock on your door this morning?"

"Yes, looking for Cree, but she isn't here. She's over her boyfriend's house... Oh wait, she just came in," she said.

Kyst would lose his mind if he knew his lil' innocent Cree had a man.

I hung up the phone when I heard glass breaking; it was coming from the basement.

"Bro, did you hear that?" Jacob asked.

"Yeah, it came from the basement. That's where Kyst's bedroom is."

I grabbed a bat out of the closet by the door and Jacob grabbed a butcher knife. He pushed me to get me to go down the stairs first.

"Chill out, pussy!" I whispered.

We lived in a bad area since the drug dealers had trap houses set up on every corner, drawing in the neighborhood fiends. We had five break-ins over the course of six years. There was a huffing growling sound coming from Kyst's bedroom.

"Whoa, what in hell is that smell? It smells like old ass," Jacob said.

I saw Crackhead Pete bumping into the wall. We called him Crackhead Pete because there are a lot of Petes in the neighborhood, so every Pete had a different name. He just so happened to be a crackhead. Kyst's window was broken, along with the bars that were put on the window to make it hard to get through. Crackhead Pete's face had open sores.

"Yo, Pete. You got to get the fuck up outta here!" I said to him. He rushed towards me, knocking me onto the stairs.

"Get the hell off of me!" I shouted. Green liquid dripped over his chapped lips and his eyes were milky white. He was snapping at me, trying to bite me as I fought him off—he was too strong. Jacob grabbed him around the neck then slammed him into the wall. Crackhead Pete got up, sniffing the air like an animal.

"He's like a crackhead power ranger!" I shouted when he tripped over a chair, trying to get to Jacob. I swung my bat at him, knocking him into the wall.

"What is going on down here?" my mother asked, coming down the stairs. Crackhead Pete jumped up and I hit him with the bat again.

"What is that smell?" she asked.

"Get back, Ma!" I shouted.

Crackhead Pete charged into me again, slamming me into the wall. He tore my shirt open with his teeth. I yelled for Jacob to stab him.

"I'll kill him!" Jacob said.

My mother tried to get Pete off of me and he sank his teeth into her hand. Jacob smashed him upside the head with a lamp, but he didn't flinch. We all fell onto the floor. Crackhead Pete was on top of my mother as she screamed. I picked up the knife and stabbed him in his neck. He was still alive. Jacob picked up one of Kyst's football helmets then struck Crackhead Pete across the head, cracking part of his skull but he was still alive. I snatched the helmet from Jacob when he bit my mother's face. I swung it at him until he stopped moving. My mother screamed when his brains dripped onto her night clothes.

"Oh my God, oh my God!" she trembled. I rushed to check her wounds. They weren't as bad as I thought. Jacob helped me get her off the floor.

The door to the basement burst opened. A tall man wearing a hoodie covering his face ran over to Crackhead Pete's body. He kicked the body twice, I guess to see if he was dead. The man pulled his hoodie away from his face.

"I knew you weren't dead! I fucking knew it!" I said, staring into my brother's face. I pulled him in for a hug and he was freezing cold. He hugged me back, squeezing me until my feet were off the ground.

"I missed y'all so much!" he said. My mother wrapped her arms around us both.

"My baby. I prayed and prayed that you weren't dead," she cried.

"Kyst is back!" Jacob said, giving him a dap hug.

"There's a lot of people like Crackhead Pete running around. I'll explain later but pack a bag of clothes. We've got to go," Kyst said.

He went into his closet and grabbed two duffle bags to fill them up with clothes.

"Tell me what's going on now! I'm happy to see you but how did you get out?" our mother asked him.

"I'll tell you later, but we have to go!" Kyst replied.

"I need medical attention. I was bitten twice, and Lord knows what kind of germs he has," our mother said. Kyst stopped packing.

"Bitten twice?" Kyst asked.

Our mother showed him her hand which was bleeding but the bite mark on her face was barely visible.

"Don't worry about that. Grab what you can before this city is completely raided with flesh-eaters. Where is Camren?" he asked our mother.

Flesh-eaters?

"She is living with her father now. We're close to being homeless," she responded.

"Okay, now go! Don't worry about Crackhead Pete, he was dead anyway," Kyst said.

"I'll help you," Jacob said to our mother. He picked up the knife before following her upstairs.

"Bro, what do you mean flesh-eaters? As in zombies? The Walking Dead type of zombies?" I asked, not believing it.

"Except these ones aren't slow nor look like dead George Washingtons. They're fast and can detect a human's scent a mile away from the slightest sound. I'll explain the rest in the truck so go get your shit before you get left," he said.

I ran upstairs to pack up, but I didn't believe Kyst one bit.

He's not the same Kyst. Maybe he's suffering from PTSD from being in jail. Yeah, that's what it is. Zombies aren't real! Besides, drugs can make people turn crazy especially if they have mental problems like Crackhead Pete.

I went into my bedroom, changing my clothes. I grabbed a backpack and put my most important things inside. I grabbed another backpack for my clothes.

"I can't leave you," I told my two-foot-long ball python.

I put him in a pillowcase then ripped a hole in it, small enough so he wouldn't slide out but big enough for him to breathe.

A noise was coming from the front door downstairs.

"Come on, Ma!" I said. Her and Jacob were rushing out of her bedroom with a duffle bag. We rushed downstairs and the front door flew open. It was the police.

"Get down on the floor now!" an officer shouted after our door was kicked in.

Damn there's a dead body in the basement.

"You can't just barge into my fucking house!" my mother said.

"We got a call that there was a break-in and from the looks of it, you two are stealing," the officer said to me and my mother.

"There's a misunderstanding," Jacob said.

"Sir, are you alright? Did anyone harm you?" the officer replied to Jacob. They had their guns pointed at me and my mother. How in the hell could we break into our own house?

"This is our house! We can take whatever we want!" I said.

"We got a call saying a black man climbed into a window and there were screams coming from this house. If this is your house, you have nothing to worry about," the officer said smartly.

"Do you mind if we search the house?" another officer said. A dispatcher's voice came from one of their walkie-talkies about a woman being attacked by her neighbor.

"Sounds like y'all have more important shit to take care of!" I said.

"Get down on the floor or I'll shoot!" one replied.

"We need to do what they say so we can make it out of here alive," my mother said.

"Ma, you better not lay on the floor in your own house. They are violating our rights," I said. We had our pictures all over the walls of our house; they were looking right at them.

"I'll go look around," a cop said.

Kyst came out of the basement and they pointed their guns at him. An officer called for backup over his radio.

What is wrong with him? Why are his eyes a different color? And why does he have green veins moving around in his face?

"Back away!" an officer shouted at Kyst.

"Get out of here!" my mother said to Kyst.

Kyst was growling, making the same noise as Crackhead Pete.

Awww shit. This nigga is smoking that stuff, too?

Kyst's body was like a flash as he moved quickly towards an officer. Blood squirted on the curtains when he bit a chunk out of a cop's neck, chewing his flesh. Bullets ripped through Kyst's body as he ate the man. A bullet struck his face, opening up his cheek. The green veins in his face pulled together, healing the wound.

My brother is a zombie!

"Get out!" Kyst said to us.

He attacked another cop, ripping through his torso. Jacob dragged my mother to the basement when military men ran towards our house.

"We've got to leave!" I shouted at Kyst.

"Get the fuck out!" he said to me. I rushed towards the basement door and Cree was coming up the stairs, wearing all black carrying a shot gun.

"My truck is by Mrs. Francis's house. Go there!" she said to me. A bullet went past my head, knocking our family picture off the wall. Cree shot back, blowing an officer's brains out.

"Grab my bags!" Kyst shouted at me.

I jumped down the stairs in the basement. Jacob was down there with my mother, trying to get her to leave. I told Jacob to grab Kyst's duffle bags as I dragged my mother out of the basement door. The loudness of Cree's shot gun vibrated against the walls.

"My son is back there," my mother said as we ran down the alley.

"Your son is a zombie! Those muthafuckas are probably dead by now!" I shouted as we ran. Mrs. Francis, an old church lady, lived a few blocks over. She used to take all the kids to bible study in her church van before she became handicapped.

"Hurry up!" I heard Kyst shouting.

I looked behind me and he was holding Cree's hand as they ran. Since nobody was chasing them, I assumed they handled the men that came into the house. I was out of breath when we made it to the back of Mrs. Francis' house. It was an old house that was barely standing up. Cree's Ford Escape was packed with duffle bags in the trunk. I tossed our bags in the back anyway before getting in the backseat. Cree's grandmother was sitting in the passenger seat, looking around in confusion.

"When is someone going to tell me what the hell is going on?" her grandmother asked.

"My baby is home," my mother responded.

SOUL Publications

"Kyst?" Cree's grandmother asked.

"Yes Kyst," my mother replied.

A girl with braids that I'd never seen before was frantically looking around in the driver's seat.

"Are you okay to drive?" I asked her.

"Just put your seat belt on!" she said.

Cree and Kyst made it to the truck, he was covered in blood—the officers' blood. Cree's grandmother screamed at the sight of him. I put my hand over her mouth.

"Just shut up and don't say shit!" I said, keeping her from bringing unwanted attention.

"We all won't fit," Kyst said.

"You... you can ride with me. You all can hide out at my parents' vacation home," Jacob stuttered. He was shaken up after witnessing Kyst eating someone.

"Okay, let's roll out," Kyst said to Jacob.

"I'm so sorry Nanny that I dragged you into this, but this city is about to turn upside down and I can't leave you behind," Cree said. I pulled my hand away from her grandmother's mouth. Rather than respond to Cree, she said a prayer instead.

"I'm going to send Isiah the address so you all can meet us there," Jacob said.

A black van pulled up in the alley. Jacob, Cree and Kyst took off running, cutting between a house. The van drove past us and Cree's grandmother breathed a sigh of relief.

"How can y'all trust that white boy?" the girl in the driver's seat asked.

"We just do, now drive before another van pulls up!" I said to her. She put the truck in reverse, backing away from Mrs. Francis' house.

"Who is that man breaking into Mrs. Francis' house?" Cree's grandmother asked. A flesh-eater knocked down Mrs. Francis' back door.

"It's a flesh-eater," the driver said. She drove out onto the road, making a sharp turn to avoid driving in the direction of the military vehicles that were driving towards the direction Kyst ran.

"Gillian, you better tell me why my granddaughter dragged me out of the house. And I hope like hell she didn't do all of this for a fugitive," Cree's grandmother said.

"It's bigger than that," Gillian replied.

"How big?" my mother asked.

"Me, Kyst and the others were in Rockstone. They were bringing prisoners there, even people who were getting locked up for petty charges. Kids were there, too," Gillian said.

"How did the children get there?" Cree's grandmother asked.

"I don't know! I just know they had us in cages for days. A lot of people were there before us. Anyway, they were experimenting on black folks to see what kind of flu vaccine can kill us off. Kyst happened to be one of their experiments. They injected him with the F-virus, but it backfired because now he has super strength and his body heals fast. I might be pushing it, but those military men aren't our men. I heard a lot of them speak when I was in Rockstone and they sounded Russian. The government sent them here to quietly do their dirty work. They want to kill us all," Gillian said.

"What's new?" my mother asked.

"There has to be a reason why all of a sudden they're trying to kill us off."

"Reparations! It's got to be that. Three months ago, they passed the bill to give us what was owed to us from our ancestors being slaves. After that, I noticed the increase of hate groups targeting us, along with the police. The government is controlling them all I bet," I said.

"That doesn't make sense," Cree's grandmother butted in.

"If this country gives all the money we're owed, they'll go further in debt. If they kill us off or kill most of us, it'll save them money. Think about it. The government put a hit out on us," I replied.

"All I know is that we need to fight back. I saw a lot of my friends die at Rockstone. If it wasn't for

Kyst helping us escape, I wouldn't be here. The government's karma is Wolfsbane," Gillian said.

"Who in the hell is Wolfsbane?" Cree's grandmother asked.

"Kyst's new name. He's not the Kyst that you all know anymore," Gillian said.

"No shit," I replied, and my mother cut her eyes at me from cursing. I remembered that she was bitten.

"How is the virus spread?" I asked Gillian.

"When you're bitten," she said. I looked at my mother's hand and she pulled her sleeve down.

"What are the symptoms?" I asked Gillian.

"Fever, rash and blindness from what I know," she said.

"That's a bunch of bull to me and I'm going to get to the bottom of it, as soon as I see Cree. She knows I'm too old for all of these crazy theories. I should've gotten her help after she lost her parents. The drug dealers in our neighborhoods are more of a threat than the government," Cree's grandmother said. We came to a traffic jam because the road ahead was blocked off. My phone beeped in my pocket and it was a message from Jacob, sending me the address to his parents' vacation home.

"They are safe!" I said in excitement.

I gave Gillian the address and she put it in her GPS. The hideout spot was five hours away.

"We can't make it there. It's traffic everywhere," Gillian said.

"Take a back road. They always get closed down last," my mother replied.

"How are you feeling, Ma?"

"I feel fine. I'm just happy that my son is free," she said.

"He's not free if the police want him, Natalie," Cree's grandmother said.

"He is free and he's unstoppable, I saw it with my own eyes. There was a reason God gave him that strength during a time like this. You read the bible, you should know that he's like our Moses," my mother said.

"I didn't think of it that way but you're right," Gillian said.

I grabbed my mother's hand and she smiled at me.

Gillian made a U-turn in the middle of traffic as cars blew their horns at her. She headed towards the countryside where it was mostly field areas, that we could ride through in case we needed to. The truck was silent as Gillian drove past a corn field. Corn fields were scary as fuck, especially at nighttime after watching Children of the Corn movies. I picked up my pillowcase that was on the floor to check on my snake, but it was empty.

"Everyone remain calm if a snake brushes past your legs," I said. Gillian screamed as if someone was killing her.

"I'm scared of snakes! Why does every hood nigga want a snake but hate rats!" she screamed.

"Yo, chill the hell out and focus on the road!" I shouted at her.

"I think it's underneath the gas petal!" Gillian yelled. I reached to the front to take control of the wheel as everyone panicked, but we ended up going into the woods. I held onto the seat as our bodies plunged forward, speeding down a steep hill, crashing into a stream. Gillian climbed out of the truck and I reached to the front to grab my snake. Cree's grandmother was slapping at my shoulder, yelling for me to throw it out.

"I'm going to throw it on you if you touch me again! Keep your hands to yourself!" I said to her.

"Respect your elders! What is wrong with you?" my mother asked. I put my snake back inside the pillowcase. Gillian was standing outside the truck having a breakdown.

"Are you okay, Ma?"

"Yes, baby, I'm fine. Don't worry about me," she replied. Cree's grandmother was on her phone; I was wondering if she was going to call the police, but whoever she was calling line was busy.

"Come on, Gillian. We have to bounce," I said.

I got out of the truck; her arms were crossed as she pouted. I was able to see all of her and she was pretty.

"Get rid of your snake," she said.

"Stay out here then. I'll drive."

"Noooooo," she said, running towards me. She wrapped her arms around me. "I need someone to hold me. I need someone to love me so we can go against the world like Cree and Wolfsbane. Can you be my apocalypse boyfriend?" she asked, looking up at me.

Shorty is bugging!

"Shorty, I'll be your husband if that means you'll bring your ass on."

"Fine!" she said.

With your cute ass.

We got into the truck, and I held onto my snake so it wouldn't cause another distraction. Cree's grandmother was still trying to make a call. I didn't trust her, and her attitude towards my mother had always been fake.

She might get us jammed up. She doesn't care about nobody but her own ass. I know bringing her with us is going to end badly but what can I do? She's an older woman and wouldn't survive by herself if we kicked her out of the truck. Besides, it's Cree's grandmother, that'll be too shady especially since Cree saved me from getting shot back at the house.

"The tire is flat. We won't be able to make it back on the road. We're stuck down here," Gillian said.

"Park the truck behind the bushes so we can hide it. We have to find shelter until we hear from Kyst," I replied.

My mother went into her purse, pulling out a Glock that I didn't know she had. She gave it to me along with bullets.

"Why are you giving me this as if you're not coming with us?" I asked her.

"If something happens to me, I want you to be able to protect yourself and others. You're a man now, Isiah," she said.

Another tire blew out when Gillian drove over tree branches. The truck stopped; we couldn't go any further.

"What is that?" my mother asked, pointing.

I looked in the direction and it was a small house in the middle of the woods.

"We can hide inside," I replied.

"I'm not going into someone else's house," Nanny said.

"We don't have a choice," Gillian replied.

We got out of the truck; Nanny was still in the passenger seat. Gillian held onto my arm as we headed towards the house. My mother picked up a stick. "I don't like this. We should've stayed in the truck," my mother said.

"We can't be trapped inside a truck, Ma. At least we can barricade ourselves in the house."

We crept up to the house, and I pulled open the door in the fence. My heart was beating in my chest walking up the stairs. The steps creaked underneath my shoes. I told Gillian and my mother to wait outside while I checked it out. The door was cracked. I was a gamer and most of the games I played were horror. A cabin in the woods was never a good sign.

I was quiet walking into the house. It smelled of mildew and burning wood, but other than that, it was a tidy cozy place. I checked out a bedroom inside the house and I almost jumped out of my skin when I heard a noise. Before I left the bedroom, I grabbed a pillow off the bed in case I had to fire my gun. I followed the noise that was coming from behind a door. A rotten smell caused my eyes to water when I pushed the door open. In the middle of the kitchen floor was an old white man eating his dog. I was careful to not make a sound; I didn't want to distract him.

Love On The Brain   Natavia

This is it. I have to kill another man, but he's not a man anymore, right? He's a flesh-eater.

I tip-toed towards him, my stomach formed in knots while hearing the sickening sounds of him chewing through the dog's stomach.

I've got to get this over with. I can do this.

I held up the pillow behind his head. He pulled away from the dog, sniffing the air; the flesh-eater picked up my scent. I shot him in the back of his head through the pillow to shield the noise from attracting others. He fell face forward, on top of his dog.

"I knew you had it in you," a voice said from behind me. I turned around and my mother and Gillian were standing in the doorway.

"I told y'all to wait outside."

"You were taking too long," Gillian said.

"Where's Nanny?"

"She's in the living room. The old bird changed her mind about sitting out there alone," Gillian replied.

"This man was infected, so there might be more in the area. We have to board up the windows, but we have to be quiet while doing it," I told them.

"Take the lead, lil' daddy," Gillian said, flirting with me.

I checked my mother's forehead and she had a normal body temperature.

"I'm fine, Isiah. I'll be back, I have to check up on Nanny," she said. She stepped closer to me. "You better watch out for that fast-ass girl. This world is too fucked up to bring babies into it. I'm warning you," my mother whispered.

"I'm a virgin, Ma," I lied.

"Umm hmm," she said, before leaving the kitchen. Gillian was in the doorway, blinking her eyes while blowing kisses at me.

"Shorty is that supposed to be sexy?"

"Wait, it doesn't turn you on?" she asked.

"No, it looks like you're infected. Were you bitten?"

"You have a smart mouth just like your brother. Anyways, I'm not touching that man or that dog," she said.

"This wanna-be relationship is ready to end already. Get your ass over here and look for a trash bag!" I said to her.

"Okay, hubby, I was just joking," she said.

This is why I prefer girls a little older. Girls my age act too bougie.

I pulled the man's body towards the back door in the kitchen. I kicked his body outside, and we went sailing to the mud.

"Why do white people like living in the woods?" Gillian asked while searching the cabinets.

"They have nothing to fear like we do."

"I found the trash bags, but I can't reach them," Gillian said. I reached over her head to grab the box.

"You play sports, too?" Gillian asked.

"Naw, I was never into sports. I like music, science and video games."

I found a pair of yellow rubber gloves that was on the counter.

"Hold the bag open," I told Gillian as I put on the gloves. She gagged when I grabbed what was left of the German Sheppard, dropping it inside the bag. Afterwards, I grabbed towels and cleaned up the floor using bleach to get rid of the rotten scent.

"This is the beginning of an apocalypse. Soon, everyone will be flesh-eaters," Gillian said.

"And we will survive it. You've just got to be strong."

"Love will defeat this," Gillian said.

"Cree told you that didn't she? It sounds just like her."

"Yes, Cree might overthink a lot, but I get it. Love will keep us together and give us something to fight for. That's why scary movies always end with a surviving man and woman in love," Gillian said.

"Nowadays, the women in those kinds of movies survive alone and they always have to be more of a fighter than the men, so kill that theory."

"Such a hater," she said.

I tied the bag up then tossed it out the back door alongside the dead flesh-eater.

Nanny and my mother were sitting on the couch when me and Gillian went into the living room.

"My phone is dead," Nanny said.

"Mine is, too," I lied.

"What are we supposed to do? I don't understand why I'm here with people who are going to jail for breaking countless laws," Nanny said.

"For right now we have to cover up the windows," Gillian replied.

"I'm not doing anything! I want to go back home," Nanny replied.

"Do you not understand how serious this is? How are you a church woman and so damn evil? There are flesh-eaters roaming around and I'm sure you cannot outrun the fast ones. Sit still, shut up and listen to what Isiah is saying. I told you that I was at Rockstone therefore I know what the hell is going on and you don't! And we didn't break the law, the law failed us, therefore we need to survive!" Gillian said to Nanny.

"You all are going to hell," Nanny said.

"This is hell," my mother replied.

"I'm going to lay down for a bit. Don't disturb me," Nanny said. She got up off the couch then went into one of the bedrooms. I pulled out my cellphone and had one service bar. My message didn't go through when I texted Jacob, telling him we were stranded.

"Can they track us through the cellphone?" Gillian asked.

"Shit, you're right."

"It's too late now. They might know where we are," Gillian said.

"I doubt they are looking for us. We can leave tonight or tomorrow morning. Where is your family, Gillian?" my mother asked.

"They are in Virginia but I'm not close with them. Most of them are alcoholics and crackheads. I came to Annapolis to live with my older cousin, but she moved to Atlanta with her boyfriend a month ago. Cree is the only family I have," Gillian said.

"You are a part of this family now," my mother replied.

"You hear that, boo? I'm your wife now," Gillian whispered.

"If you say so, shorty," I chuckled.

"You sit and rest, Ms. Natalie. Me and Isiah will make sure those flesh-eaters don't find a way in," Gillian said.

"I can rest later," my mother said, getting up from the couch. I was worried about her even though she didn't look sick, but that could change.

Come through, big bro. I hope you find us because we might not make it without you. Our mother needs you!

Wolfsbane
Peter Marks

Meanwhile...

We ran down an alley, cutting past a rehab center, looking for a safe place for the time being. For more than an hour, we'd been running from Dr. Richmond's men, police and flesh-eaters. Smoke got into Cree's eyes from a convenient store on fire. I picked her up because she was slowing down. Jacob was, too.

"Yo, I told you to go home!" I said to Jacob.

"It's too late for that! Flesh-eaters are everywhere!" he said.

A man inside the convenient store was screaming for help. Through the glass window I saw four flesh-eaters eating him.

"We have to go somewhere and chill for a few hours," I said.

"We're almost near the building my grandmother is in charge of. I have the keys in my pocket. We can use one of the church's vans," Cree said.

"It's safer to travel on foot. We'll get jammed up in a vehicle, especially if we get stuck in traffic."

"Not again!" Jacob said, when a group of flesh-eaters ran towards him. I hauled ass to keep Cree out of harm's way.

"Speed it up, Jacob! Pretend you're on the field!" I said, running through a parking lot of a nail salon. I looked back and two flesh-eaters were on our heels.

"Shoot them, Cree!"

She put the gun over my shoulder as I ran with her, cradled in my arms.

Bow! Bow!

Cree fired off the shot gun. I didn't think Cree had it in her to carry around a sawed-off shot gun, but she was nice with it.

"Holy shit! She got them down!" Jacob said, looking back.

"We're almost there. Make a left!" Cree said.

I heard a round of bullets being fired off, followed by explosions. People were running for their lives down the street. I saw a building with two church vans parked on the side.

"It's right there," Cree said.

I jumped over the fence; Jacob had to climb over it.

"Bro, I'll rob a bank if I had your abilities," he said after he landed on the ground. Cree went into her pocket, pulling out a key ring with over twenty keys. We walked around the building, going to the back door that was out of street view.

"It's quiet around here. Finally, I can breathe," Jacob said. He was leaning forward, trying to catch his breath.

"What key is it?" Cree asked, fumbling with the keys to unlock the door.

"Found it," she said, unlocking the door.

"What is this place?" Jacob asked Cree.

"For the youth. It's an after-school program for struggling parents," Cree said.

She deactivated the alarm before it went off.

Cree dropped to the floor after turning on the light switch. I pushed a heavy bookshelf across the floor to block the door. Jacob was searching the office area for water. The inside of the building was setup like a basement with green plush floors, couches, a kitchen and a large flatscreen TV. I checked the other door in front of the building to see if the metal door was sturdy. Jacob went inside the hallway closet.

"Found bottles of water," he said. He grabbed three bottles, but I told him I didn't need it.

"I'll find you something to change into," Cree said, getting off the floor. I was covered in the blood of the men I ate back at my mother's house. A piece of skin fell out of my hoodie when I took it off.

"As crazy as this might sound, I'm glad that you're alive despite the circumstances. If you gotta eat ten men, so be it," Jacob said, looking at the skin on the floor.

I went inside my pants and pulled out the folded file of papers I took from Rockstone.

"What is that?" Jacob asked, sitting next to me on the couch.

"I don't know yet, but I do know the doctor was trying to escape with them."

I flipped through the pages and there were sheets of the victims they experimented on. Every file I came across had the word *Turned* stamped across their pictures.

"What does this even mean?" Jacob asked.

"These are the people that were experimented on. Instead of the vaccine killing them, it turned them into flesh eaters."

"This file says, *Deceased,*" Jacob said.

I took the paper from him. I turned a page and it had my name written on it. Attached to the paper was a photo of me lying on a gurney in the morgue. My eyes were wide-open, blood coming out of my mouth and nose, and I had bruises on my skin from the torture I suffered while incarcerated. My cheeks were sunken in from not eating and my lips were blue. I was the only man in history that could see his own death photos. My jaws tightened as I thought about how my family would've reacted to seeing me that way. Those scientists killed me and lied about it, telling my family I died from a virus.

"Brooo, I'm really sorry that you and your people had to go through this," Jacob said. Cree came back into the room. "I found a janitor suit. It'll do for now," she said.

She sat the jumpsuit in front of me on the coffee table. "What is that?" she asked. I handed her the picture and she turned away from it once she realized what it was.

"How long do we have to stay in here?" Jacob asked.

"Until the sun goes down, it's easier to maneuver around in the city," I replied. He pulled out his cellphone to check his messages; he didn't have any missed calls.

"I hope our family is okay. I'm pissed off we got split up," Cree said.

"Trust me, Isiah will make sure they're straight. I have faith in him."

"I just hope he puts all of his gaming tactics to use," Cree laughed a little. I could see it on her face that she was afraid and probably clueless as to what she'd gotten herself into.

"There's a shower in the back. You should take one to get the grime off of you," Cree told me. She pushed open a door that had bunk beds and play pens. A picture on the wall inside the room caught my attention.

SOUL Publications

"That's Armani and Kashawn," I told Cree.

"Yes, I know them. They went missing two weeks ago. Kashawn and Armani were in a foster home funded by this church. It's called Caring Hands," Cree said.

"I saw them at Rockstone. Armani was bitten and Kashawn stayed with her. I think the church your grandmother works for was selling the children."

"Are you saying Nanny knew what they were doing?" Cree asked.

"I'm not saying that, but you can't trust her until you know for sure she didn't know anything about this."

"You know she would never do such a thing. She cares about the community just as much as I do," Cree said.

"People lose faith in what they believe in for money. I saw it with my own fucking eyes, shorty. Yo, a black man took me to Rockstone and collected money from it. He didn't give a fuck about me and the others that look like me. Like him. The police aren't the only enemies we have, Cree. Our people can be the enemy, too. Your grandmother knows something. How can kids go missing from her program and it doesn't raise a red flag?"

"I won't believe it until I have proof," Cree said.

I let it go because who would want to believe their grandparent was selling kids to a science lab? The bathroom light came on when I walked in. I looked at my reflection in the mirror and I had blood covering my face. Cree was standing behind me, raising up my shirt. She helped me out of it, her warm hands brushing across my back.

"You have the same marks as Peter," Cree said.

"School me. I know it's a story behind that."

"Peter was a runaway slave who was whipped close to death after he escaped John and Bridget Lyon's plantation in Louisiana. When he joined the Union Army, he showed his back during a medical examination. He had thick raised welts and strafe marks that crisscrossed his back. The scars were so bad, the image of his back helped turn white Northerners against slavery and helped fuel the fires of the Civil War. The green veins that cover your back, look almost the same as Peter's," Cree said. I turned around, looking at my back in the mirror. The veins there were thicker than any other veins I'd seen in my life.

"Look what they did to me. It makes me so fucking angry, Cree. I fucked up; I should've let that cop kill me that day. Death is everywhere, literally running up and down the street. I don't know what to do anymore. I should've been out there protesting with you instead of partying and pretending like our issues would fade away. This is my karma, I can feel it."

Cree cupped my chin, forcing me to look at her. "What you won't do is take the blame for everything, and what do you mean you should've let that cop kill you? I don't care what you are, you still give me butterflies because nothing's changed," Cree said.

"I should be helping my mother put up Christmas decorations right now. My mother was bitten; she probably ate everyone by now and my little sister is six hours away with her father and I don't know if I'll ever see her face again. I can't pretend like this shit doesn't hurt."

Cree wiped away the tear that fell from my eye. She grabbed a washcloth out of the closet and a towel. I took off my pants and Cree turned her head when my dick slapped against my leg.

"You were touching it when you thought you were dreaming and now you're scared?"

I took off her sweater then unclasped her bra while she covered her eyes.

"Yo, you're shy for real?" I asked.

"Yes," she replied.

I turned the shower on. The stand-up shower reminded me of the one in prison. First, I let the water run down my face, rinsing the blood off my body. The shower curtain slid back and Cree stepped in with me; she was naked. My dick hardened from lustfully staring at her juicy perky breasts. It'd been a minute since I had sex. Cree kissed me when she saw me at Kejuan's crib and there wasn't any sign of her being infected so I assumed I wasn't contagious. She backed away when I grabbed her, palming her voluptuous ass cheeks. A moan escaped her lips while I licked her neck. Shorty was loving me while I was at my worst—she was one of a kind. The sound of her heartbeat gave me a bigger erection. I didn't want to eat her, but her warm body against mine was euphoric. Her scent was driving my monster insane!

"Jacob is in the room by himself," Cree whispered when I rubbed my hand between her slit.

"He's safe. I'll know if someone comes to this building. All I need is a slice of heaven before we go back out into the world."

She relaxed as I toyed with her nipple while massaging her pussy. I used to have wet dreams about Cree. The moment was highly anticipated, and I couldn't hold back. She moaned "Wolfsbane" while I fingered her. Her tight pussy gripped the tip of my finger as her sticky warm nectar coated the outside of her mound. Cree's scent of arousal was teasing me. I couldn't wait.

"Can I come in?" I asked her. Her eyes fluttered with her mouth gaped open when I rubbed her clit with my thumb.

"Ummm yessss," she said.

I picked her up and she wrapped her legs around me. With one arm holding her up, I used my other to guide my dick between her slit. Cree held on tightly to me when I poked at her entrance with the tip of my shaft. Her body was tense, and her legs tightened around my waist. Cree deeply inhaled from the width of my dick separating her walls. I licked between her breasts, pushing upwards to ease the pain. She said she wasn't a virgin but it sure the hell was feeling like it. I was giving her slow thrusts, working my way to the pot of gold at the end of her cave.

"Ohhhh babyyyyy," she moaned into my ear. Her pussy was getting wetter, soaking wet. I held in my nut so that she wouldn't think I was a one-minute man, but her pussy was lethal, and I needed more. Her back was against the wall as I raised her legs, spreading them so that I have easy access. Sexy sounds came from her when I slid in a few more inches. The palm of my hands kneaded her buttocks while I pumped into her. Her breasts bounced as our skin slapped together.

SOUL Publications

"Fuuckkkkkkk Cree. Damnnnnn," I gritted. Her pussy put a death grip on my dick when I made her squirt. I pulled out of her then rammed my dick back into her, making her legs shake. She was getting wetter, exploding on my dick. Maybe it was too much dick for her because she couldn't take it. She screamed when I pounded at her spot.

"Hold on, baby! It's been a minute!" I said.

"I can't take it!" she said.

"You want me to stop?"

"Noooo, go deeper," she said.

I pressed my body into hers, going balls deep.

"I can't stop comingggggg," she panted. My dick was beating against her spot like a heartbeat. I fucked her against the cracked tile with a lot of built-up frustration.

"I love youuuuuuuu!" Cree screeched when I came inside of her.

Love On The Brain   Natavia

The light bulb in the bathroom blinked. Cree's body turned cold—ice cold.

"CREE! Get up!"

I lowered her body to the floor.

"CREE!"

Her body was stiff like she'd been dead for hours.

"Shorty don't do this to me now! Cree, get up!" I shouted. Even though I knew she was dead, I felt for a pulse anyway and there wasn't one. I held her close to me, rocking her back and forth.

"I told you I was a monster. I'm no good for you. Why didn't you just walk away? You shouldn't have come with me!"

Jacob rushed into the bathroom with Cree's shot gun.

"Yo, what happened?" he asked.

"She's dead."

"Is she going to turn? Did you bite her?" he asked. I ripped the shower curtain off the rod to cover up her body.

"Hell no, I didn't bite her. Look, bro, I never asked you for anything and you've been a loyal friend through it all. Shit, you're here with me now when you're supposed to be home with your family. I really need a favor from you, just this one time."

I ran my fingers through Cree's wet hair while I caressed her cheek. She looked like a sleeping angel lying in my arms. Tears fell from Jacob's bloodshot red eyes.

"She was a good person," he said.

"I know and there's nobody else like her. I had big plans, man. My goal was to play pro football and get my family out of that crack-infested neighborhood. I was going to take Cree with me, too. I've been in love with this girl since I was nine years old. I can't leave her like this by herself, so I want you to shoot me in the head."

"WHAT!" Jacob said.

"I can't do it myself. Either that or I'll attack you and force you to shoot me."

"I'm not shooting you, bro. There's no fucking way! Maybe she'll turn and wake up a flesh-eater. We have to find out first. You just can't end your life! We have to tell the world what the government is doing to black people. You think Cree would want this? Just think about it! She'd want you to expose those scientists. Come on, bro, think!" Jacob said.

"Yo, let me be alone with her."

"Take all the time you need. I'll look for a bible so we can send her off the right way," Jacob said before he left out of the bathroom. I was guilty of taking Cree's life, and letting her die alone was cowardly.

What should I do?

Cree

The Land of the Forgotten

I stood in the woods of a graveyard wearing a white lace dress.

How did I get here?

I looked around the dreary place I used to have nightmares about when I was a little girl, but in order to dream you have to be asleep. Last I remembered, Wolfsbane and I were making love in the shower.

"You're back," a woman's voice said from behind me. I turned to face her. She smiled at me with soulless black eyes, wearing a bloodstained old brown dress. The rope around her neck dragged across the ground as she walked over to me. I sat on a rock and she kneeled in front of me.

"I haven't been here in a long time."

"Because your grandmother talked you into turning your back on me. You stopped believing in this world," she said.

"She thought I was crazy when I told her about you."

Beth was lynched in 1910 by a white mob because her husband punched a white man in the face after he was spat on. The graveyard I was standing in was of spirits that were brutally murdered and didn't get justice. It'd take ten lifetimes to read each tombstone.

"This place is so cold," I said, shivering.

"It's time, Cree," she said.

"Time for what?"

"For the gift that has been waiting for you," she said. My eyes were focused on the rope she had around her neck. I reached out to get it off of neck and her blood drenched the tips of my fingers.

SOUL Publications

"I can't change how I died. The rope is stuck there," she said with blood tears falling down her face.

"What is the gift I'm supposed to have?"

Four little black girls stood behind Beth; one little girl was carrying a wooden box.

"Open the box and you'll see," Beth said.

"Do it, Cree," the little girl holding the box said.

My heart couldn't take being in the hidden graveyard. I was traumatized from it when I was a little kid.

"Take the box, Cree," Beth said. The little girl handed me the box and I took it. I opened it and inside was a ring with a black stone.

"That ring belonged to your great-great-great-great grandmother. She was the voice for the dead and saw the wicked in people's hearts. You were destined to have it," Beth said.

A young black man on a horse appeared next to Beth. He had a bullet hole the size of a tennis ball in his chest that I could see through. Beth wrapped her arms around him, and her face lit up with a smile after he pulled her up on the house—it was her husband.

"We're going back now," Beth said.

The horse ran away with Beth and her husband and the four little black girls evaporated. I put the ring on my finger...

When I opened my eyes, Wolfsbane was cradling me while resting his face on my chest.

"Please forgive me," he said with a hurt-filled voice.

I mushed him. "What did you do?" I asked. Wolfsbane pulled away from me.

"I was in here speaking in tongues and trying to catch the holy spirit to bring you back," he said.

"Bring me back from what?"

"You died and went stiff as a board. You didn't have a pulse and your body was cold," he said.

"I didn't die, fool, I crossed over."

"You a flesh-eater? All you have to do is say you're hungry and I'll bring the fattest muthafucka in here," he said.

"No, that's not what I meant. I had a dream."

"My dick game must've been trash if you fell asleep. I thought that was the only thing on me alive, but I guess that's dead, too," he said. I burst out laughing.

"Get your ass up, shorty. I was ready to die over you," he said.

"Be for real," I replied. I pecked his lips and he had tears running down his face. I wiped them away, but they were still coming. He thought I died.

"I'm serious as a preacher on Sunday. I told Jacob to shoot me or else I was going to make him do it. Baby, I was ready to be with you forever. We would have been two ice cubes in a coffin," he said. I pulled my arms from under the shower curtain that was wrapped around my body; we were sitting on the shower floor with the water still running.

"What's this?" Wolfsbane asked, grabbing my hand. I was wearing the ring Beth gave to me.

"All this time I thought they were just dreams."

"What are you talking about?" he asked, moving my hair away from my face.

"When I was younger, I used to dream of dead people. There's this world where our people who were murdered can't rest because they are forgotten. Their spirits are trapped because they can't move on. A lot of them come from slavery. That's why I buried myself in our history so I could feel their pain. From what I just learned, this ring is a gift from my ancestors to see the evil in people. I don't know how it's supposed to work."

"We'll figure it out. I always believed in spirits, especially when I saw the silhouette of my father on my sixteenth birthday. He was standing in the doorway of my bedroom and when I rubbed my eyes, he was gone, but I knew it was him. I wonder if the flesh-eaters still have their spirits. I feel a tinge of sadness when I have to kill one," he said.

"Flesh-eaters are created from science, but spirits are from God. I think the flesh-eaters still have their spirits until their brain is destroyed."

"You might be right," he said, kissing the back of my hand.

"I found a bible!" Jacob said, running into the bathroom. He dropped the bible on the floor when he saw me.

"Is she a flesh-eater?" Jacob asked.

"No, I put her to sleep, that's all," Wolfsbane bragged and I elbowed him.

"I...I saw her, bro. There's no way she was alive," Jacob said.

"We're straight. Can you give us some privacy for a few minutes?" I asked. Jacob looked at Wolfsbane for approval.

"We'll be out," Wolfsbane told Jacob. He left the bathroom, closing the door.

"He might be scared being out there by himself," I said to Wolfsbane.

"You're right," he replied.

We took a quick shower then dried off and got dressed. I found an old sweatsuit that was a little snug on me, but it was cleaner than my clothes. Wolfsbane was wearing a janitor's suit that actually looked good on him. He had definitely filled out in his arms and shoulders.

"What's on your mind?" Wolfsbane asked as we headed towards the lounging area.

"Nothing," I blushed.

"You are looking good and I'm out here looking like I'm ready to go back to a jail cell," he said.

Jacob was sitting at a table looking at his cellphone. He looked stressed out and he had tears in his eyes.

"You straight?" Wolfsbane asked him.

"I can't get in touch with my parents. What if they're dead?" Jacob asked.

"Let's not think the worst. We've got to have positive energy," I said.

"I guess you're right. My dad has a lot of weapons so I know he can defend himself. It's really my airhead mom that I'm worried about. The way my dad hates her, he probably fed her to a flesh-eater," Jacob said.

"Any word from Isiah?" Wolfsbane asked Jacob.

"None. The phone service is pretty bad now," he replied.

Wolfsbane sniffed the air, which was my cue to grab my shot gun. Jacob grabbed his butcher knife off the table.

"Don't tell me those things are close by," Jacob said.

"No, it's a human," Wolfsbane said.

He left out of the room and we followed him down the hallway towards the main door.

"Open the door! Please someone help me!" a woman shouted. She was banging on the door of the youth center.

"We have to let her in," I told Wolfsbane.

"Please, someone open the door!" the woman banged.

Wolfsbane unlocked the deadbolts on the door. A black young woman who looked to be in her mid-twenties came into the building wearing a nurse uniform. She fell against the wall, holding her chest.

"Thanks so much for letting me in," she said.

"How many were chasing you?" Jacob asked her.

"Seven I think but I lost them. There are so many people out in the streets eating each other. Hey, aren't you that football kid that killed that cop?" she asked Wolfsbane.

"No, that's not him," I said.

"Anyone have a bottle of water?" she panted.

"Were you bitten?" I replied.

"No, you can check me if you have to," she said.

"I'll get the water for her. You two might want to check to make sure she wasn't followed," Jacob said to me and Wolfsbane.

"There's no flesh-eaters around here," Wolfsbane said.

"What's your name?" I asked the woman when we went into the recreation room.

"Latisha. You look really familiar. I think we go to the same church," she said.

"Probably so. Are the police still out on the streets?"

"Yes, getting eaten by people with the virus. I've never heard of a virus that makes people eat each other," Latisha said.

"Do you have a cellphone on you?" I replied.

"No, I was robbed. People are committing crimes since law enforcement can't do anything. It's too many people running wild," she said.

"This isn't good at all. We'll be here forever," Jacob said.

"We cannot stay here for long, especially with the crime rate so high," Wolfsbane said to Jacob.

"I live five minutes away, but I know I can't make it there right now," Latisha said.

"We're leaving as soon as the sun goes down," I replied.

"I need to take a nap. I won't make it if I don't," Jacob said, lying across the couch. I picked up the papers Wolfsbane took from Rockstone before Latisha saw them.

"I think it's the end of the world. I saw an elderly man being ripped apart by a gang of crazy looking people with cloudy pupils. I'll never be the same after this," Latisha said, and I agreed.

"Take a nap, too, Cree. I'll be on the lookout," Wolfsbane said.

"Okay."

I laid at the bottom of a bunk bed to rest my body, but couldn't sleep, trying to figure out what was so special about the ring on my hand.

I'm a Medium? That's what it has to be. I can connect with the spirit world.

I wondered if my gift came from my father's side of the family. There were so many questions I needed answers to.

Since Wolfsbane is technically dead, it might've connected me back to that world again. Was it the sex? I know that when two bodies are spiritually united, we take a piece of their soul. Wolfsbane is the gate to the spirit world?

I laid on my side and Wolfsbane was in the doorway watching me.

"Shorty, go to sleep. I promise you're going to regret it. You don't know when you'll get another opportunity," he said.

"I want another teddy bear."

"I gotcha, this time I'm going to tape my death photo to it," he joked.

"When we stopped at the farm earlier and you said you had to pee, did you eat an animal?"

"No, I ate the farmer," he said.

"I'm serious."

"I am, too. I ate him while he was milking a cow. Are you going to dump me or something?" he asked with a sexy smirk.

"No, I won't dump you, but can you control it? Will me, Jacob, your family and my grandmother be safe around you?"

"Yeah I can control it. I still have a conscious."

Wolfsbane sat next to the bed, his eyes glowed when I touched his cold cheek, sending shivers up my spine.

"I'm still going to be loving on you when you turn into one of those zombies in Michael Jackson's Thriller video."

"Yoooooo, you are foul for that. Check this out though, my choreography is going to be on point if that time comes. But on a serious note, I didn't mean to get rough with you in the shower," he said.

Babbyyy, you did your thing!

"It was amazingggg," I sang while blushing.

"Go to sleep," he said.

I closed my eyes, but I couldn't sleep because I was thinking about my grandmother. Wolfsbane thought my grandmother was in on kidnapping children and although I kept my feelings to myself about it, there was a possibility that she knew what was going on.

"My heart breaks for my people but sacrifices have to be made in order to survive this world."

I reminisced on her telling me that as she prepared breakfast. My heart broke into a million pieces thinking of the woman I loved dearly being a traitor—a murderer.

Is this what Beth meant when she said this ring will allow me to see the evil in people's spirits? I have to find Nanny and see.

****

It was finally dark outside; we'd waited around for hours for our chance to leave. Jacob was cutting up cardboard boxes and duct taping it around his arms, legs and stomach. He put a piece of tape around his neck, too.

"Bro, why are you looking like you're about to be on The Wizard of Oz?" Wolfsbane asked him.

"So, I won't be easy to eat. You should do the same, ladies," Jacob said to me and Latisha.

"I can't go out of there barehanded. Do you have another gun?" Latisha asked me.

"Here," Jacob said. He gave her a spear that he made with a broom stick and a butcher's knife.

"Aim for the head. That's the only way to stop them," Jacob told Latisha.

"I'm a nurse. I save lives, not destroy them," she said.

"Shorty, they aren't human anymore," Wolfsbane told her.

"He's right. The flesh-eaters are dead already; the virus is what's keeping their bodies functioning," Jacob said.

"I don't know about this," Latisha said.

"You can stay here, just know nobody is going to come for you. The government is behind this genocide. This whole area is predominately black and Hispanic so we're on our own. They don't give a fuck about you, so you don't have a choice but to kill if you don't want to die. We can't babysit you," Wolfsbane told her.

"Is he always this rude?" Latisha whispered to me.

"Yeah, he doesn't bite his tongue."

"I'm ready!" Jacob said, slapping his stomach.

"Bend your knees, bruh," Wolfsbane told Jacob. Jacob couldn't bend his knees because he pretty much taped them together. I poked Jacob and he tipped right over.

"Maybe I overdid it," Jacob said.

"How is the virus contracted?" Latisha asked.

"Saliva from the infected," I replied.

"So, it's like rabies?" Latisha asked.

"Yes, but way more aggressive," I replied.

Wolfsbane strapped my fanny pack around my waist which had my shotgun bullets inside. He was beginning to treat me like a baby, but at least he was thoughtful.

"You don't need a weapon?" Latisha asked Wolfsbane.

"No, I'm good," he replied, putting on a backpack filled with bottled waters.

"I'm ready," Jacob said, loosening the tape.

Wolfsbane pushed the bookshelf away from the back door. He opened the door, going first.

"Aight, the coast is clear but there's a lot of smoke outside so stay close. Cree, I'll carry you," Wolfsbane said.

Latisha smacked her teeth; she was getting on my nerves and I wanted to curse her out.

"Is there a problem?" I asked her.

"Actually, it is. I'm a woman, too, so he needs to be more respectful. I'm lighter than you," she said.

"My sister, my sister, please don't make me turn against you. Once you get on my bad side, that's it," I replied.

"Let it go, baby," Wolfsbane said to me.

I can't stand prissy bitches! I should've left her ass outside!

I took the backpack from Wolfsbane since he had to carry me on his back. The smoke was strong when we left out of the building, wherever the fire was coming from was very close. I pulled up my coat to cover my nose.

"I don't sense any flesh-eaters, so we should be good until we make it out of the city," Wolfsbane said.

"We have to walk Latisha home," Jacob said.

There was a car turned upside down hanging halfway out of a laundromat. A pickup truck with the American flag on the back, pulled up to a corner store. A man leaning out of the passenger window threw a Molotov through the corner store's window. The ring on my finger stung my hand; I blew on my finger, shaking my hand to cool it off.

I think this ring is trying to warn me of those men.

"Burn this nigger city down!" a man yelled from his truck.

"The noise they're making is drawing the flesh-eaters. They will be here soon," Wolfsbane said.

The burning sensation on my finger went away when Wolfsbane ran between two buildings, coming to a dead end. Latisha yelled for us to make a right to go to her house.

"It's a dead end. We'll have to go around to get to the other side," Jacob said.

Wolfsbane crawled up the wall of the building.

"Whoaaaaaa," I said.

"Hold on, Cree," he said.

It was a tall building, probably standing close to twenty feet. He climbed onto the roof. He told me to stay put while he went back down to get Jacob and Latisha. From where I was standing, I could see the flesh-eaters running towards our street because of the noise coming from the pickup truck. There were so many of them, I didn't have any more hope.

We're not going to make it out of this.

The flesh-eaters were getting closer to the pickup truck. Wolfsbane brought Jacob and Latisha up to the roof. I rolled my eyes at Latisha because she was holding on to my man with her legs wrapped around him.

"It's safe up here. I'll be right back," Wolfsbane said.

"Where are you going?" I asked.

"To take care of something," he replied. He jumped off the building, into the dark alley.

"He's strong," Latisha said about Wolfsbane.

"And he's mine before you get any ideas," I replied, and she rolled her eyes.

"Where do you think he's going? It's freezing up here," Jacob said.

"I'm not sure but I think I know," I replied.

I saw Wolfsbane creeping up the sidewalk, going into the cloud of smoke. He was heading towards the pickup truck.

He's going to eat those racist pieces of shit!

Wolfsbane

The Ring

A group of white men was destroying the businesses in the neighborhood. With the city being shut down, everyone had to fend for themselves. Someone was spray painting a barber shop window with the word *Niggers* in bright orange. He was ready to write another word; I grabbed his arm, snapping it in half. He fell to the ground, holding his dangling arm.

"Get away from him, motherfucker!" a middle-aged man said with his gun pointed at me.

"Y'all are a bunch of cowards. Where was this energy before the virus started? Drop the gun, bitch, and fight me!" I replied to the gunman. Another pickup pulled up to the barber shop packed with white men armed with military weapons. One of the men jumped off the truck carrying a noose.

History ain't repeating itself today!

"I'm going to hang you from the light pole for what you did to Paul!" the man with the rope said to me.

"We run this city now!" another man said.

"Shoot him, Bill!" a man shouted.

A bullet pierced through my chest and another through my skull. I stumbled back from the impact.

A bullet to the head and I'm still alive. I cannot die.

"Is this nigger bulletproof? Shoot him again, Bill!" someone said. Multiple bullets rippled through my body.

"Stop shooting!" the man shouted as my body pushed out the bullets to heal.

"I think he's one of those things," a man said.

"No way, he would've been dead by now," someone replied.

"UGGGGGHHHHHHH!" A man shouted as I took a chunk out of his neck. Bill ran towards the truck to get away. I dropped the dead man on the ground to chase after Bill; Bill dropped his gun when I tackled him.

"Please don't kill me! I'm sorry!" Bill cried.

A mob of flesh-eaters came running from behind the buildings, a couple of them crawling out of storm drains. I tore into Bill's neck, devouring human flesh. I stopped eating when a flesh-eater dragged Bill away from me. A horrific scream echoed throughout the sky when a man's body was pulled apart by the flesh-eaters. They were ripping him like paper. When his intestines spilled out onto the street, a little girl rushed to it. The red sweater she was wearing looked familiar—it was Armani. A flesh-eater pushed Armani and took the meat from her. In the crowd was people that I knew, five of them I went to high school with. A man ran down the street yelling for help. He almost got away, but a flesh-eater knocked him through the window of a check cashing place.

I went to a pickup truck and collected three guns along with bullets. There was also a hunting knife between the seats covered in blood...human blood.

Those pigs were out hunting innocent lives I bet.

Someone underneath the truck grabbed my ankle.

"Please help me. I'll take you to the safe place. I have a wife and kids," the white man begged. If I had to guess his age, he looked to be in his late fifties.

"Safe place?"

"Yes. Yes... A safe place. It's in Eastern Shore, as soon as you get off the bridge. This is an infected zone, so they won't let anyone out of it. You are trapped here unless you come with me. I didn't kill anyone; I promise I didn't. I only tagged along. I've been hiding here since we arrived," he whispered.

"Is that right?"

"Absolutely. I know you want to get out of here," he replied.

"Death is a return; we leave life how we come here and today is your day," I said.

I dragged him from underneath the truck by his hair.

"Nooooo, please don't!" he cried.

Armani was sitting on the ground while the others around her ate. I brought him to her. The man pleaded with his eyes for me to let him loose, but I didn't feel sorry for him. He shrieked when Armani bit a chuck out of his head, eating his brain. Although she was a little girl, she was too strong for him to get away as she held him down, biting through his cranium. A flesh-eater ate the man's fingers, others joined Armani, eating his limbs. She growled at an infected firefighter when he pulled the body away from her—she scared him off.

This will buy me time to get Cree, Jacob and Latisha out of this area.

I climbed up the wall of the building with the guns strapped around my back. My body was changing, growing stronger. Every time I ate human flesh, it boosted my metabolism.

I'll probably look like Tales from the Crypt if I don't eat. Fuck that! Cree saying she'll love me through whatever, but I know she ain't going to stick around for that.

I pulled myself up on the ledge of the roof. Cree was sitting down staring at the ring on her finger.

"What happened to you?" Latisha asked, grabbing my face, examining me. I was covered in blood, saturated in it. Cree bumped her out of the way when she came over to me.

"I was only examining him. You can back the fuck up," Latisha said to Cree.

"Hoe, you running up to him like he's here for you!" Cree said.

"Chill out, Cree. Latisha is a nurse and it's a good thing to have one around. She doesn't know Ky—I mean Wolfsbane can heal on his own," Jacob said.

"Check this out, Latisha, keep your hands to yourself. You're too touchy feely and I have a problem with that," Cree told her.

"Sis, you're tripping if you think I'm that easy," Latisha said.

"Whoa, where did you get these from?" Jacob asked when I handed him a gun.

"I found it in a pickup truck."

"I'm good with my baby right here," Cree said, holding her shot gun.

"I can save these for Isiah."

"Speaking of Isiah. A text just came through from him. He said he's in a cabin in the woods by Route 301. I don't know how long ago he sent it because after it came through, I lost service again," Jacob said, handing me his cellphone.

"He didn't say anything about our mother or Cree's grandmother so they should be safe," I replied.

"I hope Gillian is safe too," Cree said.

"We'll make it there in a few hours if we stay focused," I replied.

"There's an exit door on the roof. We can get to the other side by going through this building," I told everyone.

I knocked down the emergency door on the roof.

"I think the building is empty," I said.

"All these stairs," Latisha said.

"You ain't lying," Cree replied.

Love On The Brain Natavia

I picked Cree up to take her down the stairs. Jacob told Latisha not to think about asking him because he couldn't make it down himself.

"How many did you eat?" Cree asked me while resting in my arms.

"Just one. Are you uncomfortable with me being drenched in blood?"

She went into her coat pocket, pulling out a napkin. She wiped my face off.

"I didn't want any in my hair," she said.

"I'm exhausted," Jacob complained.

"Bro, how did you make the football team? You can barely run, and you get tired quick."

"College parties and beer," he said.

"How old are you two?" Latisha asked.

"I'm twenty-one and Wolfsbane is twenty," Jacob replied.

"Did your mother name you Wolfsbane? It's a cute and weird name," Latisha said.

"Yeah, that's my name," I responded.

"How old are you?" Jacob asked Latisha.

"Twenty-five," she replied.

"You're beautiful by the way," Jacob responded.

"Is Jacob trying to holla at Latisha?" Cree asked me.

"Probably, he loves the sistas," I chuckled.

Five minutes later, we were on the last floor. We walked out of the building and the street was pretty much clear except for the four police cars that were on fire.

"My house is right there on the end," Latisha said. I put Cree down since she wanted to walk. Her stomach was growling from not eating.

"You need to eat something," I told Cree.

"Food is the last thing on my mind. I'm worried about our family and friends," she said.

"I'll find you something to eat," I replied.

We reached Latisha's house and there was blood on the fence. The front door was wide open with blood on the porch. Latisha ran into the house and Jacob followed her, leaving me and Cree on the sidewalk.

"Owwww owwww. It burns!" Cree said, holding her hand. She was pulling at the ring on her finger.

"Shorty, what's wrong?" I asked, trying to see what was happening.

"It burns," she said.

I couldn't pull it off either, it was stuck on her hand.

The streetlight flickered the same way it did when me and Cree was having sex in the shower. Her skin was getting cold—freezing cold. Her pupils turned; her eyes were the same color as the stone on her ring. I thought she was tripping when she told me she crossed over while we were in the shower and got the ring from her dream. When she went cold and stiff, I was thinking it was my doing, but seeing her eyes turn made me realize that she could've been telling the truth.

"They were killed by the men in that pickup truck with the knife you took," Cree said. She was zoned out like she was under a hypnosis—she was communicating with the dead.

"Who?"

"Latisha's parents and grandmother. They're standing in the doorway," Cree said.

I didn't see anyone but Latisha and Jacob looking around. I took the hunting knife out of my pocket and remembered there was blood on it when I took it.

"Their bodies were dragged out of the house and put on that truck," she said. I looked on the sidewalk and saw the bloody streaks of someone being dragged. There were a lot of them.

"Latisha's father wants us to look after her and he's thankful that she found us. Had she been home, she would've been dead, too," Cree said.

Latisha was sitting on the porch crying, trying to figure out where her family went.

"Her mother doesn't want her to know about them. We can't tell her," Cree said. Tears fell down Cree's face after her eyes turned back to their original dark brown color.

"I don't want this gift. I shouldn't have taken this ring. It's so pitiful how we're treated like this! I can't take it!" Cree said. I wrapped my arms around her, hugging her tightly.

"This is their karma, shorty. Dead people are walking the Earth because their hate influenced them to fuck with science, creating a virus that's going to destroy them, too. You have an amazing gift because now their stories will never be silenced. Do you know what this means? Innocent victims can tell you what happened to them. You are the voice—their voice."

"I'm overwhelmed," Cree said.

"You have to come with us, Latisha," I told her.

"But my family. You think they could be infected?" she asked.

"They could be, but you can't stay here. Grab whatever you need but don't be more than ten minutes. Jacob, you go help her," I said.

Jacob followed Latisha upstairs to help her pack whatever she needed. I stood on the sidewalk with my arms wrapped around Cree. It was crazy how life worked; me and the girl I loved were both connected to the dead. She was my soulmate.

Isiah

Cabin Fever

Three hours later...

I sat up on the couch in a daze. Looking around the small living room inside the cabin, I wished my surroundings were different. Being inside the house in the woods reminded me of the horror I'd witnessed. I stretched my long legs, yawning while being pissed off that I fell asleep even though I was exhausted from boarding up the house.

"Ma!" I called out.

I got up and searched. The door to the room Nanny was using was halfway open. I knocked before peeking in. She was sitting up in bed reading the bible.

"You seen my mother?" I asked her.

"I've been in this room since we got here," she said, flipping the page.

I closed her door then checked the other bedroom. Gillian was hanging off the bed with a towel wrapped around her body. She moved closer to the edge; her towel exposed her meaty ass cheeks. I quickly went over to her to keep her from falling off the bed. She jumped up and was ready to scream, probably thinking I was a flesh-eater before she noticed me.

"Don't do that! You scared me!" she said.

"My bad. You were ready to fall on the floor. I'm in here because I can't find my mother. Did she say anything to you before she left?"

"Last I saw her, she was in the kitchen drinking a glass of water," Gillian said.

I went into the kitchen for the second time and noticed there was a note on the counter. My head was pounding from an instant headache as I read the note...

Love On The Brain   Natavia

I know you're wondering why I left but I was beginning to feel sick. I didn't want you to see me like that, this family has been through enough already. Don't come looking for me. Do not risk your life to find me. Stick with your brother every step of the way and go wherever he goes. Protect each other. Since Camren is in New York with her father, she should be safe but check up on her if you can. I love each and every one of you. Take care Isiah. I'm gone now...

I crunched the letter up, tossing it in the sink. Gillian came into the kitchen fully dressed.

"What happened? Where is she?" she asked.

"She's gone. She left because she was feeling sick. Why didn't she wake me up? I shouldn't have gone to sleep. I'm always fucking up."

I picked up the letter out of the sink to hand it to Gillian. She unraveled the paper and read it.

"She didn't look sick to me. I was the last one to fall asleep and she was sitting in the kitchen drinking water, talking to me. She told me to take a shower and a nap and she'd wake you up if she heard anything. I checked her and she didn't have a fever. According to the time on the wall, that was only forty minutes ago," she said.

"Fuck this. I'm going to look for her."

I went into the living room to get my gun, but it was gone.

I know she didn't take my gun. Something fishy's going on around here.

I went into the kitchen looking through the drawers for a knife or something else I could use for a weapon, but I couldn't find any.

"I'm coming with you," Gillian said, putting on a coat.

"You stay here."

"No, I'm not staying here with that old bitch. She gives me bad vibes," Gillian said.

"Aren't you scared of the flesh-eaters? Don't put yourself in a situation that you don't have to be in. If my brother finds us, I want you to tell him what happened to me and my mother. Stay put and if you hear anything, hide under the bed.

Don't scream if you see one, it'll draw more of them."

"Okay, hurry back," she said.

Gillian pecked my lips; I wasn't sure if she meant to do it or if she was only feeling me because she didn't want to be alone. Whatever it was, I wasn't complaining.

"Stay put."

"Here, wear this," she said. She took off the oversized coat and gave it to me.

I opened the back door, stepping out into the night's crisp air. There was an axe in the middle of a tree stump. I pulled the axe out of the stump before leaving the front of the cabin. An Asian flesh-eater was walking in circles in the middle of a stream, sniffing the air for food. He grunted and squealed when he caught a whiff of my scent. I gripped my axe tightly as he ran towards me. I swung across his neck, cutting his head off. His body fell into the stream, but it was still moving while his yapping head flowed downstream.

That was gross as fuck!

I ran up the hill that we'd come down when Gillian crashed Cree's truck. When I came out of the woods, I was on a main road. A flesh-eater was smashed flatly on the ground like roadkill. A lot had changed since the morning, because the world looked completely different. A car was stuck between two trees with a disfigured body hanging out. I ducked behind a tree when a black truck rode past.

What am I doing? My mother is long gone and is probably a flesh-eater now. There's no way I can find her, but I can't give up.

All of sudden, a flesh-eater came out of the woods, tackling me to the ground. She snapped at me with her bloody teeth as I reached for the axe that fell out of my hand. I couldn't get a clear view of its face, but the hair was similar to my mother's; I didn't want to kill it. The flesh-eater held me down, ripping the fabric of the coat I was wearing. I managed to push it off and realized it wasn't my mother. It lunged at me again and I picked up the axe, splitting the flesh-eater's skull.

"Damn that was close."

I hid behind a tree when I heard someone moving from behind a bush across the road. It was chilly out, but I had sweat beads running down my forehead. I was nervous being out at night by myself with infected cannibals—I was scared shitless.

A flesh-eater crawled out of the woods and a bullet wisped past its head. The second bullet went through the flesh-eater's head, killing it. Five emerged out of the woods, they were hit with a riddle of bullets before making it across the road.

My mother is gone. I can't make it farther than this.

Whomever was shooting and killing the flesh-eaters possibly already killed my mother. I headed back towards the cabin, feeling like a loser. My mother told me I was no longer a boy and that I had to man up, but I couldn't cross that road for her. I wasn't supposed to give up so easily, but I did. Tears burned my eyes but it was too cold for them to fall down my face; the tears froze to my cheeks instead. A Caucasian boy flesh-eater was walking into a tree. He looked no older than eight. He had a puss-filled bite mark on his neck and reeked of a distinct odor. I killed him, putting him out of his misery.

Gillian was waiting for me at the kitchen table when I made it back to the cabin. I sat in the chair across from her.

"Did you get bitten?" she asked, looking at the hole in the sleeve of the coat.

"I couldn't do it. I didn't make it far. What am I supposed to tell Kyst about our mother? He trusted me to protect her."

"When someone gives you their final wishes, it is best to keep their best interests at heart. You weren't supposed to go looking for her. She told you not to. Here, eat this," she said. Gillian pushed a bowl of canned soup across the table towards me. She also handed me a towel and told me to wipe my eyes.

"Having a girlfriend during a time like this ain't bad at all," I said. I changed the subject to avoid talking about my mother. The way I saw it, she could still be alive.

"I told you it's the best way to survive. Give me the spoon, I'll feed you," she said.

"I'm good."

Gillian kicked my leg underneath the table.

"You've got to start being nice to me," she said.

"I am nice to you."

"Nooo, I want you to be touchy feely," she said. I almost choked on my soup when she said that.

"My family is broken up and you think I have that on my mind right now?"

"It'll take your mind off it. Tomorrow isn't promised. We have to go out with a bang. You know, when I was back at Rockstone, I felt in my heart that we weren't going to make it. There's the government then there's just us. You think we can survive like this? We're pretty much already dead. I don't want to die a virgin," she said.

Oh boy.

"Yo, you serious about all of this? I was playing along with you. I don't want you to give it up so easily."

Gillian crossed her arms after she scooted away from the table.

"My whole name is Isiah Asari Macklin. I'm eighteen years old and my favorite color is red. I'm allergic to flowers and I love animals. I lost my virginity three years ago and I never had a girlfriend before."

"I'm Gillian Marie Alexander. I'm nineteen years old. I love pink and I'm scared of my own shadow sometimes. No known allergies and I've had ten boyfriends, but they dumped me because I'm a virgin," she said.

"We know each other a little more now."

"I see what you did there," she said.

I finished the soup then stood from the table. Gillian told me to take a shower since I smelled like a flesh-eater. I did smell a little foul. I brought our bags in from Cree's truck earlier before I took a nap. After I grabbed a sweat suit, socks and boxers I went to the bathroom. Gillian came in behind me to bring me a bar of soap from the closet. The bathroom was too small for two people. My body was pressed against hers.

"I'll set your axe by the door," she said. I grabbed her arm, stopping her from leaving.

"Thanks for everything."

"You're welcome," she blushed.

She left the bathroom, closing the door. I peeled off my clothes and noticed a mark on my arm from when the flesh-eater attacked me in the woods. It was a bruise from when she bit through the sleeve of the coat. I was relieved it didn't break any skin. When I stepped into the shower, the water was ice cold. It was painful taking a cold shower in the winter inside of a house with little heat. While rinsing the soap off, I heard a loud noise and Gillian yelling. My body was soaking wet when I stepped into my sweatpants. I grabbed the axe by the bathroom door.

SOUL Publications

"Get your hands off of me!" Gillian said. I ran into the living room. Four men dressed in all black carrying guns were inside the cabin.

"Put the axe down or I'll shoot," a man with a Russian accent said to me. I dropped the axe on the floor.

They were probably the ones shooting the flesh-eaters in the woods.

"Where is your brother?" a black man asked. He was the same man I saw in the van with Detective Jamison.

"I don't know, and I wouldn't tell you anyway!"

A man with a scarred face grabbed Gillian by her braids, yanking her to her knees. He pulled out a knife and held it against her throat.

"He'll kill that bitch if I tell him or you can watch them have their turn with her," the black dude said.

"You on their side? Black as you are and you siding with them muthafuckas? Yo, don't you see what they did to the city? What the fuck is wrong with you?" I asked. The agony I had in my heart almost stopped it from beating.

"Your brother said the same shit to me when I transported him to Rockstone. You think we all need to stick together when you ghetto ass kids ruin your neighborhoods by slinging dope, robbing old ladies and raping women," he said. The man with the scarred face punched Gillian in the face and her nose bled. I was hit in my stomach with the butt of a machine gun.

"Leave him alone!" Gillian shouted while I was being kicked.

"You said you only wanted to ask them questions! Not hurt them!" Nanny said. I spit out blood on the floor. For years I'd known she was an evil woman that hid behind her bible, and now she'd proven that to me.

"Go back in the room, Nanny," the black officer said to her. He seemed familiar with her. The only people who called her Nanny were those who personally knew her.

Love On The Brain   Natavia

"This was not a part of the plan, Derrick! Leave these kids alone," she told him.

"You boot-licking house negros! How dare you do this to us!" Gillian said. She was punched in the face, knocked out cold. I was kicked in the head when I reached for her.

"Now they know you know me. Why didn't you stay in the room?" Derrick asked Nanny.

"I want out of this, Derrick. This is the last time I betray God. I can't do it anymore. So, get what you want out of them and leave," Nanny said.

"Stop using God for this shit!" I shouted. The third man in the room shot me in the leg with a silencer.

"Where is Kyst? Just tell us where he is and you'll make it out," he said. My leg was bleeding profusely.

"We're all dead anyway. Killing me won't matter," I gritted.

"Just tell him where he is," Nanny pleaded.

"I'm not telling that nigga shit! Fuck him! Fuck all of you!"

"I bet he'll talk if we hang him up from a branch," the fourth man with a Russian accent said.

"And tell his brother it was suicide," the one with the scarred face said. They all laughed at the sick joke. Derrick clenched his jaw; I saw the anger in his eyes. He was their puppet; they were using him against his own people. Gillian squirmed on the floor; she was starting to wake up. The man with the scarred face ripped open her shirt, exposing her breasts.

"She's young, just how I like them," he said.

"I don't know where my brother is. We split up in the city," I confessed. A walkie-talkie beeped and a voice came through.

"Bring the brother to my lab...Alive!" the man on the walkie-talkie said.

"Saved by the bell. Let's go," Derrick said. I was handcuffed with my hands behind my back. My side ached when they pulled me up from broken ribs. Gillian was handcuffed, too.

"If you see Kyst, make sure you call me. Dr. Richmond needs him," Derrick said to Nanny.

"You cannot leave me in the woods. I won't last out here by myself," Nanny said to Derrick.

"I can't help you until you give us Kyst. In the meantime, lock the doors. Reach out to me on this," he replied, giving her a walkie-talkie. I was dragged out of the house, slipping in and out of consciousness. Blood was coming out of my mouth and my lungs ached when I breathed.

"I don't think he's going to make it. You hit him too hard," Derrick said to the fourth man he was with.

"You picked the wrong time to care huh, buddy?" he asked Derrick. A flesh-eater jumped out at Derrick and was shot in the head.

"We have to hurry before they follow the sound," Derrick said. I was barefoot, walking on the ground. My wounded leg dragged behind me since I couldn't walk on it.

"You and your brother think you're so tough. If you can't beat them, you have to play it smart.

You think I like doing this? I don't but I get paid a lot of money for my job. That's all I care about," Derrick whispered to me.

"You'll die before me," I said.

"Are you threatening me?" Derrick asked.

I couldn't respond, because of the pain in my side. When I fell again, I couldn't move.

"Get up, Isiah," Gillian cried.

I was losing blood and was struggling to breathe.

"We need to get him to Dr. Richmond before he dies. If he dies on our watch, we'll be executed. You know the rules," the one with scarred face said. An ambush of flesh-eaters bombarded us. Gun fire lit up the woods like the Fourth of July. I heard Gillian yell for me to get up as I closed my eyes...

****

"Can you hear me, Isiah?" a doctor asked me. I was woozy and not able to see clearly. My head, side, back and leg ached. He flashed a light in my eyes. "Can you hear me?" he asked again. I slurred while answering him.

"I gave you a sedative for the pain. Let's sit you up," he said. He reclined the hospital bed sitting me up. From what I could make out, I was in a glass hospital room with two other doctors. I wanted to rub my eyes, but my arms were handcuffed to the railing on the bed. It took two or three minutes for me to regain my vision.

"What are you doing? Why are there tubes in my body?" I asked the doctor.

"Let me formally introduce myself. I'm Dr. Richmond, me and my team came from Antarctica to do a research on the flu virus to understand the impact it has on the African-American community," he said.

Lies!

"Where is Gillian?"

"She's in the next room. You'll see her soon," he said.

"His blood also matches experiment 10569," a woman said, holding a clipboard.

"Great news. Can you all leave out of the room while I speak to Isiah?" he asked the doctors. Dr. Richmond slid his chair closer to the bed after his team left the room.

"I'm not a bad person. I was hired to do these awful things. It's how I pay to do my research," he said. He picked up a cup off the tray next to my bed. I turned my head to avoid taking a sip of the water.

"Twelve years ago, in Antarctica I met a solider who was battling a rare case of leukemia. I mean it was so rare that I couldn't figure out what it was. That was unusual for me because I was always a quick thinker when it came to the human anatomy. He let me use his body for experiments so that I could treat others in the future who had the same illness. That man was your father Isiah," Dr. Richmond said.

"The lies you insane people tell are ridiculous!"

"I saved samples of his blood and used it to make the F-virus. If you are immune the same way as your brother, you'll have the same outcome since you two carry your father's genes. Just imagine being bullet proof and even better, not being able to die," he said.

I spit a glob of blood in his face. "I don't believe nothing you just told me. My father didn't have leukemia!"

"After I give you this vaccine, I'll inject Gillian with your sperm. You should be thankful of science. The birth of a child with the F-virus will be the new beginning of mankind. You should be grateful for your special genes. This is a miracle," he said.

"You are going to get her pregnant? She's a virgin you pale-face sack of shit!" I yelled.

"Mary was a virgin, too, and she created Jesus. Think of yourself as God. Your father was a true believer of making the world a better place. This isn't anything personal. Life is about making a change even if you have to do something bad to make it better," he said.

Dr. Richmond injected me with a green liquid. My skin started sizzling like someone threw hot grease on me. He put tape over my mouth to mute the sounds.

"Don't fight it," he said.

The experience was similar to a rollercoaster. The room was spinning as I had an out-of-body experience. I silently screamed for my mother while enduring the pain of my body being set on fire. The machines I was hooked up to beeped loudly. Before taking my last breath, I saw shadowed figures surrounding me. They were spirits, welcoming me to the other side...

Cree
Secrets of Betrayal

Meanwhile...

Wolfsbane held me up while guiding me through the woods on Route 301. It took us three hours to get there on foot. My feet were hurting, and I could barely keep my eyes open. Piles of flesh-eaters were sprawled out everywhere riddled with bullet wounds.

"I can't go anymore," Latisha said. She sat on a rock, breathing heavily. I felt bad for her. I saw her parents and grandmother's spirits standing on the porch of their house three hours prior. After communicating with them, I learned they were murdered in cold blood and dumped on the side of the road, all because they'd witnessed a lynch mob beating up a homeless man.

Jacob sat down next to Latisha. "We can set up camp somewhere around here," Jacob said.

"We can rest for fifteen minutes then we have to bounce," Wolfsbane said. I sat against a tree, drinking a bottle of water.

"They cut our cellphone service off," Jacob said.

"To stop all communication. The lights will be off soon I bet if they haven't turned them off already. This city will be a ghost town by morning. Once I get everyone together, I'm leaving this place, but I really need to see about my mother. She was bitten when I last saw her," Wolfsbane said.

"So, we came here for just your mother? Can we look for my family?" Latisha asked.

She still doesn't know her family is dead, but I can't tell her.

"I didn't force anybody to come with me. Originally me and Cree was supposed to go to Texas until shit went left so don't come at me like that," Wolfsbane replied.

"We have to deal with the possibility of our families no longer being with us," I spoke up.

Latisha's mother's spirit was sitting on the rock behind her. If only she knew her family was still with her but not physically.

"What are you looking at? Do I have something in my hair?" Latisha asked.

"I'm looking at the stars," I lied. Her mother's spirit walked away, going between the trees.

"I'll be back," I told Wolfsbane.

"Where are you going?" Wolfsbane asked.

"I need to go to the bathroom."

Wolfsbane got up to go with me. "I'm okay. I want to go by myself."

"Are you sure?" he asked.

"Yeah."

He helped me step over a fallen tree log. Latisha's mother was waiting for me on the other side of the stream. I followed her until she stopped next to a bush.

"Is that my truck?" I said aloud.

I had a burnt orange truck and the back of it was peeking through the tree branches. The doors were locked. Latisha's mother disappeared after I saw a cabin sitting in the middle of the woods. The windows were boarded up, but I could see light shining through the cracks. I jumped when Wolfsbane leaped from behind a bush.

"Can you not do that?" I asked with my heart pounding.

"I heard you say, 'Is that my truck,'" he replied.

You can't say anything around Wolfsbane. His ears are too sensitive.

"My truck must've crashed down here and they went into that house."

"There's someone inside," he said.

"Just one person?"

"The scent would be stronger if it was more people inside," he replied. He told me to stay put while he checked the house. The door was halfway off the hinges when he pushed it open. I ran to the house when I saw my grandmother step out on to the porch.

"I'm okay, baby," she said when I hugged her. The ring on my finger burned my hand.

"Are you alright? You look like you're in pain?" Nanny asked.

"I'm fine," I smiled weakly.

"Where is my mother and Isiah?" Wolfsbane asked Nanny.

"Natalie, Isiah and Gillian turned. We were ambushed by so many of those things," Nanny cried. I noticed blood on the porch, the pattern the same as the ones at Latisha's house. Someone was dragged out of the cabin.

"I don't believe it. I can't believe it. Are you saying that my brother and mother are dead? Everybody is dead but you?" Wolfsbane asked Nanny.

"Who was dragged out of here?" I asked Nanny.

"There was a lot going on. I don't know. I'm grateful that you're here," she replied. A spirit of a little black girl stood in the hallway. She pointed at my grandmother.

"Get in here. It's freezing," my grandmother said. The spirit vanished when Nanny pulled me inside the cabin.

Wolfsbane was standing in the doorway. "I can't believe you, Nanny. Are you telling me that a sixty-something year old woman survived an ambush?" Wolfsbane asked her.

"What exactly are you trying to accuse me of?" she asked.

"I'm going to leave out to bring Jacob and Latisha back. When I return, her prunie ass better know something. I haven't tried an old person yet, but I'm happy to add one to the menu," Wolfsbane said.

"I can't let you talk to her like that!" I yelled at him.

"I don't give a shit about her being kin to you! My mother and brother are gone! And she got me fucked up if she thinks she's off limits. Talk to her," he said, leaving out of the door.

"Where did you get this?" Nanny asked when she grabbed my hand, looking at my ring.

"I think you know where I got it from," I replied, snatching my hand back.

"Take it off. That's voodoo, pure evil!" she screamed at me.

"It's evident that you knew all along about my gift and you wanted me to think they were nightmares so that I could stay away from them."

She pointed a gun at my head. My feelings were past hurt. My grandmother turned out to be the person Wolfsbane warned me of. I got teary eyed thinking about the sweet little lady that raised me.

"Take it off or I'll have to take matters into my own hands," she said.

"How do you know about this ring, Nanny? You've seen it before, haven't you?"

"I told my son not to marry your mother. She brought spirits into my house the first day I met her! Even with holy water, I could still feel their presence in my home. I didn't want you to be like that, Cree. It's wicked," she said.

"Were the spirits victims of child trafficking? I need to know the truth, Nanny. What all did you do? What don't you want me to see?"

"I needed the money to keep the church and I only sold children that didn't have a future," she said.

"Don't do that, Nanny. You sold them because you were money hungry! People like you are giving good churches bad names. This was all on you."

"You don't know anything! Those children were having sex, doing drugs and listening to rap music. We don't need children like that on this Earth," she said.

"Your ancestors are ashamed of you."

"The past isn't my problem! The future is what I strive for. Money is what we need to build generational wealth! That's why rich white kids have more than the nappy-headed kids in the hood. If we do what they did, we can have a house on the hill. Your children will be able to go to those fancy schools and not a school with metal detectors. So, I sacrificed the bad seeds to help our future. I have to kill you now, baby. You carry the dead around with you," she said.

She dropped the gun on the floor when she saw Wolfsbane, Jacob and Latisha standing in the hallway.

"Did you all hear me?" Nanny asked them.

Wolfsbane's eyes glowed, green veins spreading across his face like a spider's web. He huffed, reminding me of a predator. Wolfsbane charged into her with his hand around her throat.

"STOP!" I shouted.

"What do you mean, Cree? She's the enemy," Wolfsbane said.

"I want her to think about what she did. Eating her will be too easy."

"Eating her?" Latisha asked everyone.

"Wolfsbane is a flesh-eater, too. The virus had a different effect on him than the others," Jacob replied.

"I'm getting out of here," Latisha said. She ran out of the house and Jacob went after her. Nanny yelped after Wolfsbane dropped her on the floor. He looked at me in disgust.

"Where is Natalie, Isiah and Gillian?" I asked Nanny.

"I don't know," she said.

Wolfsbane went inside the bedroom, slamming the door hard enough to crack the wall.

"He's a monster," Nanny said.

"No, you're the monster! That man spared your life for my sake. Don't you ever in your life call him that!"

"You think he loves you? He loves white women. He went to jail over a white woman! Think about that," she replied.

"And you are out here selling children to white scientists. You have no room to talk, Nanny. Aren't you the one who told me that the devil speaks backwards?"

Jacob came back into the house with Latisha. She was throwing a hissy fit and it wasn't the time for that.

"This whole time we've been with a flesh-eater?" Latisha asked.

"Not now, Latisha. Jacob, can you tie my grandmother to that chair over there?" I asked. Nanny swung at me when I picked her up off the floor.

"You're not stronger than me!" I shouted. Nanny popped me in the face and pulled my hair, yelling out obscenities. Jacob broke it up, holding her arms down.

"Grab her legs!" I told Latisha.

All three of us sat her in a chair in the kitchen. Latisha went to the backpack to get rope.

"I should've performed an exorcism on you! You wicked little bitch! I raised you when I didn't have to!" Nanny yelled at me.

"Shut up!" I said.

We tied the rope around her body. She bit Latisha's arm and her dentures came out, hanging on Latisha's shirt. Wolfsbane came into the kitchen. He opened up the fridge, ignoring us struggling with Nanny.

"Bro, you can't help?" Jacob asked.

"You need help with a woman who doesn't weigh more than a deer tick? Whose teeth are on the floor?" Wolfsbane asked, leaning against the counter.

"Stop being an asshole and grab her feet," I told Wolfsbane.

"Those arthritis feet ain't hard to hold down. Jacob, you are disappointing me, bruh. You are turning red for no reason. You about one-hundred pounds heavier than that lil' head Yorkie," Wolfsbane said. My grandmother's wig came off.

"Check for bite marks. She's falling apart," Wolfsbane said. Latisha was kicked in the chest. My grandmother's legs were going everywhere. Wolfsbane grew agitated. He grabbed the chair from the bottom and held her upside down.

"We're weak. We don't have the energy," Jacob said out of breath.

Wolfsbane wrapped the rope around her legs then put her in front of the back door of the kitchen.

"That way if a flesh-eater comes in, it'll eat her first," Wolfsbane said.

"Can you please stop?" I asked.

"Shorty, I don't care about your Jesse Jackson-looking grandmother right now. She admitted to selling children, not to mention, I still believe she knows where my family went. You can baby her ass up all you want to but she's an old thug and needs to be thrown out like trash. Matter of fact, let's feed her to the children that's infected like Armani," Wolfsbane said.

"She's still my grandmother!" I replied.

A flesh-eater burst through the back door. Wolfsbane squeezed its head until it burst open.

"There's a lot of infected military men in this area," Wolfsbane said. He kicked the remains of the flesh-eater down the stairs.

"Me and Jacob are going to fix the doors," Wolfsbane said. They walked out of the kitchen, leaving me with Latisha and my grandmother.

"Does this place have a shower? I stink," Latisha said.

"You can search for one."

She left the kitchen with an attitude.

I used cable wire to make sure Nanny couldn't budge in the chair.

"You are making a big mistake," Nanny said.

"Go to hell."

Wolfsbane came into the kitchen with a board, hammer and nails.

"We can talk after I fix this," Wolfsbane said to me. He wrapped a shirt around my grandmother's mouth so that she could stop making noises. I looked around the cabin and it was small but tidy minus the blood in the living room. Bags were on the floor by the couch. One of the duffel bags belonged to Wolfsbane. Inside his bag was a picture of me and him on Halloween when we were younger.

"You weren't supposed to see that," Wolfsbane said from behind me.

"I packed a picture of me and you, too, along with that teddy bear you gave me our senior year of high school."

"That's when I was Kyst," he said.

"You were reborn to protect. This is only the beginning. As time goes on, you'll see that you are still Kyst."

"Damn it!" Jacob said, holding his finger. It was bleeding from nipping himself with a nail.

"I think I need stitches," Jacob said.

"You never used a hammer before?" I asked him.

"The last time I ate was yesterday. I'm shaking," he said.

"I'll look for something," I replied.

"I'll do it. Jacob, go rest. There's two bedrooms in here. You and Latisha can take the first room. Nobody should be in the living room. The front door is weak, but the bedroom doors are sturdier in case one of you has to shut yourself in a room for safety," Wolfsbane said. He went into the kitchen, looking through the cabinets.

Jacob sat on the couch with his hand wrapped up in his shirt.

"You should go to the safe zone. I know you'll be able to make it there."

"I'm not going there, Cree. I can't be around a bunch of hate-filled people. I'd rather stay out here," Jacob said.

"If you don't stand for something, you'll fall for anything," I replied. I found a bag of weed at the bottom of my bag along with an easy roll up. Jacob dropped to his knees.

"Thank you so much!" he said with his hands clasped together. I passed him the weed and blunt. Wolfsbane came into the living room with cans of food, crackers and chips.

"I found these at the very top of the cabinets. This should help," he said.

"Sweet, dude! I'm about to party!" Jacob said in excitement. I picked through the canned foods to see what I wanted.

"Shorty, you can't be picky. Eat something," Wolfsbane said. I took two cans of sardines in mustard sauce.

"This smells worse than a flesh-eater. I can't," I said.

"It's not bad," Jacob said, chewing a mouth full. The tangy taste from the mustard made me gag. I was hungry but not hungry enough for the food. Latisha came from the back then grabbed three cans of greens.

"You want a sausage?" Jacob asked her.

"I'm vegan," Latisha said.

"Kudos to you," Jacob replied.

Wolfsbane left the living room.

"What's wrong with him?" Latisha asked.

"He doesn't believe his mother and brother turned. I don't believe it either. Look around, you don't see any sign of an ambush. Maybe someone was injured, but I don't believe Nanny," I replied.

I got up and went into the kitchen and my grandmother was taking a nap with her head against the wall, her arms tied to the back of her chair. After checking on her, I went back into the living room.

Thirty minutes later...

I found Wolfsbane laying across the bed, staring at the ceiling. His handsome face was visible again. He cleaned off the blood that was smeared across his cheek. I closed the door to the bedroom then placed my shot gun next to the bed. Wolfsbane sat up, pulling me on his lap.

"Are there any spirits in here?" he asked.

"Not right now. You'll know when one comes around. The lights will flicker and the hair on the back of your neck will stand up as a gust of wind whistles in your ear."

"You sitting on my lap is my giving me an erection. The erections I have now as a flesh-eater are different than the ones I had when I was human," he said.

"How different?"

Love On The Brain   Natavia

"I want to do bad things to you like tying you up and fucking you until you can't breathe. Pull your hair while sucking on your breasts. I want to know if I can make aggressive love to you," he said. Wolfsbane was groping my center while flickering his tongue behind my ear.

"Can I do that?" he asked. I shook my head, letting him know that he could take advantage of me, and violate me in every way. He stood me up, slid my pants to my ankles. I was bare and wasn't wearing any panties. He put his hand between my slit, coating my pussy lips with my essence. He stood up, towering over me by inches. A whimpering moan erupted from the bottom of my stomach when his strong hands, squeezed my ass cheeks. I was so horny—too horny. He wrapped his hand around my neck, pushing me against the thin wall of the bedroom. He ripped the hoodie I was wearing, right down the middle. I was dying on the inside, needing him to put me out of my misery.

"Keep the fuck still," he gritted when I reached to unhook my bra. He simultaneously suckled at my breast and fucked my pussy with his finger. He told me if I came, he was going to bite me. I was always different, especially with my abilities, so wanting to get bit by my flesh-eating boyfriend wasn't bizarre. Plus, he wasn't contagious. I damn near cried when he sank his teeth into my nipple. My inner thighs were drenched with my cream. Wolfsbane gripped my hair, turning me to face the wall. He sat underneath me, pushing me up onto his shoulders, with my legs wrapped around his neck. My clit jumped when he French kissed my pussy, huffing like a giant grizzly bear. He was holding me under my ass cheeks, moaning loudly while eating my fruit. I couldn't take it! I was nowhere near as sexually experienced as Wolfsbane. He slid his middle finger in my rear end, punishing me for trying to control his head movements.

"You better not come!" he said against my swollen center.

"Can I come?" I whispered.

He lowered me to lie beneath him, my back on the floor, legs over my head. He had me folded like a pair of pressed jeans. I reached out to grab the leg of the bed, but he snatched my arm away. He got rougher, pinning me down, eating me out. My pussy swelled to the point it was rejecting his tongue and it angered him! He used two fingers, pumping them furiously in and out my entrance.

My mound exploded as I squealed like a pig. He flipped me over, gripped my hair tightly while smacking my ass.

"What did I tell you, Cree? Who in the fuck told you to squirt in my mouth?" he asked. His arrogant talk and hard smacks to my ass caused my temper to rise enough to warm his cold body.

"I need it! Put it inside me."

He got up off the floor, holding me. He laid me across the bed, lustfully staring at my body with his silver glowing eyes. He pulled out his dick and it hung between his legs like a horse. It was the prettiest, fattest and longest piece I'd seen in my life. I was scared but ready. He told me to slide to the edge of the bed and spread my legs. He grabbed two belts off the dresser, tying one leg to the headboard rail and my other leg to the footboard rail. I was stretched out like string cheese.

"If you tell me to stop I will, but other than that, I'm not holding back," he warned.

"I don't want you to."

He tied my wrists together with a wire. After he was done tying me down, he rubbed his swollen shaft around my opening. I was breathing heavily from nervousness and excitement.

"You got me so hard, Cree," he said, teasing me with the tip of his dick. He pushed my legs further apart, penetrating the tightness of my center. My eyes were dancing around in my head while he pummeled my pussy.

"Ohhhhhhhhh....ummmmmmph!" Hoarse moans spilled off my lips.

"Shit, Cree," he groaned. Grabbing my breasts, he twisted and pinched my nipples. Wolfsbane was in the back of my pussy, disrespectfully hitting my G-spot. Steam covered the mirror on the vanity from the heat pouring off my body. He pulled out, kissing my wet and sticky lips, eating me out all over again.

"I can't take it!" I shouted, squirting for the third time.

"You want me to stop?" he asked between licks.

"Noooooo!" I cried out.

He came back in, giving me deep grinding strokes that paralyzed my lower body. I was feeling high, overdosing off his rough but passionate love. His deep husky groans threw me over the edge. I called out his name repeatedly. The candle in the room blew out from the air seeping through the cracks underneath the window. My body orgasmed before shutting down. I heard Wolfsbane call out to me, but I was suffering from sleep paralysis...

I was in the land of the forgotten again, walking through the woods holding a lantern. It was freezing and my bare feet almost froze to the ground. I followed the loud voice of a woman singing and the tall fire that peeked over the trees from a mile away. Once I made it to the fire, I saw many women, children and men dancing around its flames. A heavyset woman was singing a song called "Let Us Break Bread Together." It was a song associated with the Underground Railroad. A young man standing next to me was clapping his hands together. He was dressed in a white hospital gown with an IV in his arm—it was Isiah.

"What happened to you?"

"Cree? Oh shit, my bad. I didn't know you were standing right here," he said. He had blood running from his leg.

"Can you tell me what happened to you, Gillian and Natalie?"

"My mother left the cabin because she was feeling sick and didn't want us to see her that way. As for me and Gillian, I think we are in a hospital. Dr. Richmond injected me with the vaccine, he says I'm immune to it, so I'll be like Kyst. Nanny knows what happened to us," he said. I wanted to ask him more about Nanny, but he faded away...

"CREE!" I sat up on the bed and Wolfsbane was looking at me.

"Did you see them?" he asked.

"I only saw Isiah and he had a leg wound. Dr. Richmond has him and Gillian. He also told me that Dr. Richmond injected him with the vaccine. About your mother, she left because she was starting to feel sick. I'm so sorry."

Wolfsbane backed away from the bed in disbelief.

"My mother turned. This is my fault," he said, sitting on the bed.

"I don't know what to say, but at least she had a chance to see you one last time."

"Deep in my heart, I knew what was going to come out of her getting infected. I guess I was in denial. The good thing is that she left before we could see her that way," he said. I wiped away the tear that fell from his eye. We were tired of crying; I know I was. I wanted everything to disappear and be back to normal because we were hurting.

"I wonder why Isiah was in the spirit world."

"If Isiah is going to end up like me, he has to die first before he can turn into what I am. I think I was dead for six days before resurrecting. I know he was afraid and in pain going through it. That injection feels like your skin is on fire and your head is going to explode. The only positive thing is that he'll be able to walk around the flesh eaters. I need to find him. I can't leave him in the hands of Dr. Richmond. That man is very cruel," he replied.

I almost lost my footing when I climbed out of the bed. My arms and legs were aching from the aftermath of being tied up.

"Shorty, where are you going?" he asked.

"To make my grandmother talk. I'm done sparing her. She might know where Dr. Richmond is keeping Isiah and Gillian."

I got dressed in a sweat suit before storming out of the bedroom. My grandmother was asleep in the chair when I snatched the duct tape off her mouth.

"Where in the fuck are they?" I yelled at her.

"Who?" she asked, confused.

"Gillian and Isiah! I saw Isiah in the spirit land, and he told me he and Gillian are with Dr. Richmond. What lab were they taken to? Isiah told me that you know who took him and Gillian!" I said.

"I don't know!" she said.

Wolfsbane came into the kitchen putting a shirt over his head.

"I say you let me eat her," he said.

Jacob came into the kitchen wiping sleep out of his eyes.

"What's up with all the noise? Keep it down so the flesh-eaters won't come," Jacob whispered.

"This bitch knows about the lab. Tell me, Nanny, tell me who are these people you are working with. You don't know what you've gotten yourself into! Tell me right now or I'll cut it out of you!" I screamed at her.

"The man's name is Derrick; he works for the government, taking on private missions. I knew he made a lot of money working for them, but I didn't know what kind of jobs he was taking on until I asked him for money to save the church and youth center from being shut down. Derrick told me that I could make the money on my own if I helped him sell people that nobody would miss. He said it was for experiments. It wasn't supposed to go this far but I got addicted to the money and couldn't stop. I thought I was doing a good thing by sending troubled people away. They were useless!" she cried. My grandmother was asking God for forgiveness as she confessed all of the crimes, she partook in.

"Who is Derrick?" Wolfsbane asked Nanny.

"He used to come to my youth center when he was a little kid. We kept in touch over the years—he's like a son to me. He worked undercover in your prison; his name is Officer Brown," Nanny told Wolfsbane.

"Officer Brown is the clown that took me to Rockstone. He hates my black ass because I killed a racist-ass cop who wouldn't have given two fucks about him. I got something for his punk ass when I see him. How can I get in touch with him?" Wolfsbane asked Nanny.

"There's a walkie-talkie underneath the floorboard under the dresser in the first bedroom. I can talk to him; I'll do anything if you'd just untie me. I'm afraid to get eaten," Nanny replied.

Jacob went into the bedroom to get the walkie-talkie; he came back with it a few seconds later.

"If you say anything out of the way, alerting him that we're on to him, what Wolfsbane will do to you is out of my hands," I warned Nanny.

"If tying you up and eating your pussy was all I had to do, I would've been done it," Wolfsbane whispered in my ear. I elbowed him, blushing it off.

"Press the button," Nanny said.

Jacob pressed the button, and nothing happened. A battery light came on.

"It needs batteries," Jacob said.

"I'll search the house," Wolfsbane said.

"Ask Latisha if she packed any batteries," I said to Jacob. He left out of the kitchen.

"You're going to die being with that boy, Cree. Those people will stop at nothing to get him back. It's not too late to turn back," Nanny said.

"And go where, Nanny? You don't get it, do you? The government doesn't give a fuck about us! The safe zone they have in Eastern Shore isn't meant for us poverty-stricken people. You thought you were helping us, but you were helping them get rid of us. Your spirit will never get through the gates of heaven. When you die, nothing of your presence will exist. As for Wolfsbane, I love him and I'm sticking by him. Those white folks won't break us up. I know how they like to snatch black men from their families. If I die for the cause, it'll be a sweet death."

"I hope he loves you the same way," she said.

"I DO! Don't worry about us!" Wolfsbane shouted out.

I keep forgetting his hearing is ten times better than ours.

He came into the kitchen. "I plan on marrying Cree, even in an apocalypse," he said. Nanny leaned against the wall and closed her eyes.

"No batteries," Jacob said.

"We'll have to make a trip to the store. I've got to get to Isiah," Wolfsbane said.

"A store? You'll get caught," Jacob said to Wolfsbane.

"I can't die," Wolfsbane said.

"Shit, we can. I'd rather get shot five times in my dick before getting eaten by a flesh-eater," Jacob said.

"Stay here and protect the cabin. I know you can do it. Plus, I'm sort of familiar with this route. I think there's a market about nine miles down the road," Wolfsbane replied.

"That's a two-hour walk," I said.

"I can run and climb trees to stay out of the way. We don't have a choice because if bullets start flying, I can't protect everybody from getting shot. There's enough guns here for everyone and if you have to run, leave me a note under the couch so when I come back, I'll know what happened," Wolfsbane said.

"I can come with you," I replied.

"Fuck no, Cree. Stay here," he said.

"What if they catch you?" I said.

"I'll make sure they don't. I'm hungry anyway and it's uncomfortable eating human flesh around you," Wolfsbane said.

"I don't care," I replied. I was serious when I said I was riding to the end of the world with Wolfsbane. If he had to eat human flesh in front of me so be it. In my eyes he was innocent no matter what because he didn't ask to be a zombie.

"That's not the point. The point is that I care, so respect it," he said. "Jacob, protect the women at all costs. If you have to sacrifice bald-head small-head in a flesh-eater ambush then do that," Wolfsbane said, referring to my grandmother.

"Okay, I gotcha," Jacob said.

"Come with me," Wolfsbane told me. I followed him to the bedroom pouting that I couldn't be his sidekick.

"Yo, you mad?" he asked.

"Yes, I want to go."

"I don't want you dying for me so get that off your brain," he replied.

"Love *is* on my brain, that's what I think about every second I'm with you."

"I have to make a confession. I came on to you that way so you could cross over. I had to know where my mother and brother went. I had a gut feeling that you were the only one who could reach them, and you did," he said.

"Since your spirit is in both worlds, it'll always be this way when I sleep with you, so don't think you used me."

"I was serious when I said I want you to be my wife. You take the coldness away from my body whenever I'm with you," he said.

"Hurry up and leave before I change my mind."

He pulled a pair of Nike tennis shoes out of his gym bag along with a black hoodie.

SOUL Publications

"Get a piece of paper now and a pen so you won't have to search for it in case of an emergency," he said.

"I will."

He pressed his forehead to mine.

"I love you," he said.

"I love you, too, now go."

He kissed my forehead before leaving the bedroom. I followed him. Jacob pulled off a piece of wood that was holding the front door together so that Wolfsbane could exit.

"Keep the women safe," Wolfsbane said.

"I will. See you when you get back," Jacob said, giving Wolfsbane a dap hug. I sat on the couch after Wolfsbane left the cabin.

"Don't worry, Cree. He'll make it back and I'll look after you and Latisha," Jacob said.

He sat on the other end of the couch. "This will calm your nerves," he said, holding a blunt towards me.

"Light it up then."

"How long are you going to leave your grandmother tied up?" Jacob asked.

"I don't know but I don't think she deserves to be free."

Please make it back safely Wolfsbane. I won't be able to survive in this without you. I'm begging you to stay out of harm's away!

Wolfsbane

The Reality

An hour later...

I got to the market sooner than I expected since I ran the entire way. I was surprised I hadn't come across any humans. The roads were jammed up because of crashed cars and dead bodies cluttering the streets. Flesh-eaters were everywhere in the area, especially in the parking lot of the market, walking around in circles and sniffing around for their next meal. I pushed a flesh-eater away from the door of the market because his wheelchair was blocking the entrance. The door and windows to the market were still intact, probably because there were too many flesh-eaters in the area for anyone to break in. I kicked the door down and the flesh-eaters in the parking lot turned towards me. Once they realized I wasn't human, they went back to walking around. The alarm went off, but I took my time so I wouldn't overlook something we needed. I came to an aisle of tampons and maxi pads and it made me think of my shorty. I'd never forget what happened to her when she was over my mother's house watching Camren. That was back when our lives were simple...

Six years ago...

Cree was sitting on the couch in my mother's living room eating popcorn while Camren scribbled in her coloring book on the living room floor. She was supposed to be helping me with our social studies project instead of watching a Tyler Perry show.

"Get over here and help me!"

"Get Ashley to help you!" Cree said. Ashley was a girl I sat next to in our social studies class and Cree thought I liked her.

"The teacher didn't assign her, she assigned us to work on this together."

"I'm babysitting," Cree said.

"How so? My mother is upstairs."

Cree smacked her teeth and I threw a pen at her.

"Why did you do that?" she asked, getting up. I jumped out of the kitchen chair and Cree chased me around the dining room table.

"I'm going to kick your skinny ass!" she said, going back to the couch.

"You have something on the back of your pants!"

"I'm not falling for that again. Last time you tripped me up in front of the class when I looked down at my shoes because you told me I had dog shit at the bottom of them. Stop playing with me before I beat you up," she said.

"I'll take a picture of it and send it to your phone, but you better see if it ain't on my mama's couch."

Cree touched her butt. "Is that blood?" I asked. She ran into the bathroom and locked the door.

"You want me to bring you a pad from my mother's room?" I asked, knocking on the door. She cracked it open, sticking her head out.

"And a pair of your basketball shorts or sweatpants. You better not tell anyone about this either, Kyst. If you do, I'm going to tell Natalie you hooked school last week," she said.

"I wasn't going to tell anybody with your honey bun-shaped head ass."

"You hooked school?" my mother asked as she stood at the top of the stairs.

"Uh oh," Cree said, closing the bathroom door.

"Hey Ma, why you ain't taking a nap?"

"Boy, get your ass up here!" she said.

"See, Big Red, you got me in trouble!"

I chuckled to myself thinking about Cree's period going through her clothes and how I got my ass whipped that day. I put three boxes of pads in a backpack along with pain pills.

"We need this, too."

Love On The Brain   Natavia

I grabbed shampoo, deodorant, hair conditioner, canned foods, candy bars and all the batteries since I never checked to see what kind we needed. The backpack was loaded, and I couldn't travel heavy in case I got jammed up with the law. I turned the knob on the door that read, *Employees Only.* The back was filled with food.

I'll have to make another trip in a few days, hopefully the flesh-eaters stay in this area, so nobody comes here.

I left the market through the back door.

"AHHHHHHHH!" a woman screamed.

"Get the fuck off!" I recognized the voice. It was my homeboy Tray. I followed the noise that came from the post office around the corner. In the parking lot was a flesh-eater pulling a woman out of a truck's window by the hair. Tray and three other guys I knew from the football team, was beating the flesh-eater with a bat. Five flesh-eaters ran towards them.

I can't let them get eaten. Shit, Cree is going to have a fit if she has to wait long for me.

A flesh-eater charged at Tray, knocking him on the ground. I intervened, squeezing the flesh-eater's head until it burst. I picked up an axe someone dropped on the ground, killing the flesh-eaters.

"Kyst? My nigga Kyst Macklin? Oh, hell nawl, bro!" Tray asked, picking me up from the ground.

"Bro, how? I went to your mother's crib with Jacob and she told me you died. How did you get out?" he asked.

"It's a long story but let's just say they can't keep a brother like me down, you feel me?" I asked.

"We were at a party a few nights ago and out of nowhere, cannibals crashed the party and started eating people. We can't get in touch with our families and the police is shooting down anyone this color," he said, tapping his skin.

"It's a genocide out here. But you have to lay low, stop drawing attention and stay off the roads. Driving around is too hot."

"My boy Kyst. I don't care what you did, you are still a part of our team and the best quarter back in the district," my friend Jeremy said.

"Glad to see you all alive," I said, giving him dap.

"We've been staying at an abandoned hotel further down the road. Want to roll with us? You seem like you know a lot about what's going on," Jeremy said.

"I like being alone. But listen, there's a lot of flesh-eaters in the front of the market, so don't go that way."

"Where you staying at, bro? Come with us so we can catch up. I missed you," Tray said.

"I'm good."

"At least get in so we can drop you off somewhere," Jeremy said. The back door of the truck opened and the girl I let ruin my life stepped out of the truck. She sprinted over to me then jumped on me with her legs wrapped around me.

"I'm so sorry for everything," Melody said. I pushed her away from me. Seeing her brought the pain back of what I had to deal with because of her racist cop father. A drunken late-night fling turned into a disaster.

"I hated my father for what he did to you and I truly and sincerely apologize for it bringing harm to your family," Melody said.

"Come on, Mel, now is not the time to bring that up," Jeremy told her.

"It's been eating me up for a while now. I take the blame for telling my father about you. My father used to rape me until I went off to college and nobody believed me, even when I acted out by sleeping with a lot of boys; nobody saw that I needed help. I know you might hate me but you're a hero for killing him. He raped my younger sister, too. He did a lot of sick and twisted shit and his friends covered up for him," Melody said.

I don't know what to say.

"I don't know where you are going, but me and my girl are coming with you. It's too crowded in that truck," Tray said. He helped his girlfriend out of the SUV, and she didn't look good.

"Was she bitten?" I asked.

"Yeah, last night. She's running a fever," Jeremy said.

"Oh shit! There they go! Everyone get in!" Jeremy shouted. A mob of flesh-eaters were coming towards the truck. Jeremy and Melody got into the crowded Expedition.

"Come on!" I told Tray. His girlfriend couldn't run, she almost collapsed standing on her own. I picked her up, dashing across the road to the woods. Tray was fast, he was the running back on our football team. The flesh-eaters were chasing the Expedition as we hid behind the trees.

"I'm so glad I got out of there. I need to get my girl to the hospital. She's losing her eyesight," he said. I sat her down, leaning her against the tree. She was developing rashes on her skin and her brown eyes were dull, ready to turn milky white. She was shivering from chills and green blood started dripping from her nose.

Love On The Brain Natavia

"Yo, what the fuck is happening to her? Andrea, baby, can you hear me?" Tray asked her.

"She's dying, bro, she's infected."

"We need to get her some meds. Come on, man, help me out. That's been my shorty since elementary school," he cried.

"There's nothing we can do for her. You either let her turn or put her out of her misery. If it was my girl though, I'd end it for her. You wouldn't want anyone to shoot her down or see her body decaying, but that's your call."

"Andrea, come on, baby, wake up!" he said, tapping her face. She was slipping in and out of consciousness.

"She's going to turn. I know it's hard for you right now, but we can't do shit about this, bro. What do you want to do, I can't let you sit here and get eaten. She won't recognize you after she turns."

Tray fell to his knees and sobbed when Andrea's body convulsed. Her arms and legs were making crackling sounds. It was my first time actually seeing someone turn and it was creepy. Andrea's eyes went completely dull after she stopped shaking.

"Get up, Tray!" I said.

"I can't," he sobbed, as Andrea sat up, her neck was jerking, making ticking sounds. She sniffed the air with a growl brewing in her throat. She opened her mouth, ready to take a mean bite out of Tray's face. I raised the axe, cracking her skull right down the middle. He screamed when her dead body fell into him.

"Nooooooooooo!" he cried.

"Get your ass up, Tray! What is wrong with you, bro? Next time I get hungry, I'm going to remember that you want to be a flesh-eater's dinner."

"You killed my girl!" he said, tackling me and slamming me against the tree. I backhanded him.

"Slap out of it—I mean snap. You touch me again, I'm going to forget we're homies."

"I'm dreaming, got to be! How else would I be talking to a dead person? Slap me again. Wake me up," he said. I slapped him and he fell next to Andrea's dead body. The rotten pungent stench of flesh-eaters burned my nose; they were coming for Tray.

"All that noise you made, now they're coming. I have to get you somewhere safe."

I grabbed Tray by his letterman's jacket while he snatched off the necklace from Andrea's body.

"What is that smell?" he asked.

"When it's strong like that, there's way more than one. The noise attracted them," I said. I climbed up a tree with one arm while pulling him up by the neckline of his jacket with the other. Tray hung from a branch and I told him to hang on for dear life. I picked up the axe as about thirty flesh-eaters surrounded us.

"This is going to take me all night. Sorry, Cree!"

I cracked a flesh-eater between the middle of its head then another. My arms were ready to pop out of the socket while killing them, but I had to do it so they couldn't follow me and Tray to the cabin. Afterwards, I fell to the ground with a rumbling stomach, hungry from working out.

Ba-boomp... Ba-boomp... Ba-boomp...

Tray's heart was beating too fast, he was panicking.

He slid down the tree, looking at me with wide eyes, shocked.

"You killed all of them in ten minutes," he said, looking at his watch.

"What happened to you? Why are your eyes changing?" he asked with a shaky voice.

"I'll tell you the story on our way to the cabin, but I'm giving you a heads up, I go by Wolfsbane now. The name Kyst depresses me, reminding me of good times."

I gave him the axe with gooey green blood dripping from it.

"Aim for the head. Come on," I said.

While walking deeper into the woods, I gave Tray the rundown of what happened to me over the past few months, but he didn't fully believe me.

"So, you are pretty much saying that you shift into a zombie?" he asked.

"Yeah, anger and hunger triggers that other side."

"It's fucked up what happened to you but just so we're clear, me and you aren't homies anymore," Tray said.

"Cool with me, long as you're safe."

I shrugged off Tray's attitude. I understood wholeheartedly how he was feeling over losing someone because I felt the same way when my mother and brother went missing. But unlike Tray, I wasn't in denial about the government's agenda. Denial was an ugly trait to harbor because denial lacks reality.

I hope bringing him to the cabin won't be a mistake.

I didn't have the energy to beef with a close friend for not understanding how serious the virus was when I had a list of stuff to worry about, like the world ending.

Two and a half hours later...

"Is this the place?" Tray asked when we made it to the cabin.

"Yeah."

"It's wayyyy better than the place we were staying at," he said.

I walked through the fence then up the stairs on the porch. The door opened seconds later after I knocked three times, twenty seconds apart, so Cree would know it was me. Jacob opened the door.

"Finally!" he said.

"Look who I found," I told Jacob, stepping to the side.

"My fucking brother Tray!" Jacob said in excitement.

"What's up, bro. Where's the bathroom?" Tray asked dryly, refusing to shake Jacob's hand.

"Ohhh kayyy, it's down the hall to the right," Jacob replied.

"Yo, what's wrong with him?" Jacob asked when Tray went into the bathroom.

"Andrea turned and I killed her."

"That's messed up. I can't imagine what that feels like," Jacob said. He closed the door, sliding a board underneath it so it would be difficult to open. If someone tried to come in, the board would scrape across the floor, letting us know someone entered the house.

"I found a market that was fully loaded," I told Jacob. He took the bag from me, dumping everything on the table.

"Real snacks!" he said.

I went into the bedroom and Cree was lying on the bed in a fetal position, sleeping peacefully. My stomach was aching from not eating and the thought of human food made it worse. Cree opened her eyes when she heard my stomach growl.

"You didn't find anyone to eat?" she asked, sitting up.

"No, I didn't see anyone but a couple of people I went to school with. Tray is here but he's shaken up because I had to kill his girlfriend. She was infected."

"At least he doesn't have to see her walking around like that, poor thing. You want me to talk to him?" she asked.

"No, Tray is stubborn, so he'll come around when he's ready talk about it. On our way here, I told him about Rockstone and how it changed me. He doesn't believe most of what I told him, but he'll figure out how screwed up the government is sooner or later."

My stomach growled again. These hunger pains were feeling the same as a gunshot wound to the abdomen. I stretched out across the bed and Cree kissed the side of my face. The warmth of her skin and fresh scent of her human flesh wasn't making it any better. I'd rather run far away from Cree than attack her, but this was still a tease.

"I bought you back a couple of things from the market. When I grabbed a few boxes of pads, I thought of that time you your period came through your pants. It was crazy how we were always around each other but never got along. Damn I miss those days."

"I used to write in my diary about you and boyyyyyy I was doing you dirty on those pages. You made me sick," she smiled, showcasing a dimple.

"And you always snitched on me to my mother."

Mannn Ma Dukes is gone. Me and Isiah are parentless now.

Cree covered her mouth and snickered. She was the reason why I was always punished during our high school years. I playfully mushed her, and she giggled.

"Yo, I heard what your grandmother said about me only wanting you because of the circumstances we are in, but I've always wanted you. It got to me because it sort of does seem that way but that'll never be the case. I was young and enjoying being a teenage football star. That slip-up with Melody—"

Cree pressed her finger against my lips. "I was doing me, too, so we're not going to go down that road. You don't owe me an explanation," she said.

"I saw her while I was out there and she apologized for putting me in the middle of her and her father's business. She thanked me for killing him because he was raping her and her sister. I don't feel as bad for myself as I used to knowing that I saved other women from being raped."

"You're a hero," she said.

Jacob called me into the kitchen.

"This thing is completely broken," Jacob said.

"That's bullshit. Derrick is like my son; he wouldn't give me a broken walkie-talkie. He's going to come back for me," Nanny said.

"Shut up, old hound. They used you, left you out to pickle and die. Nobody was coming back for you; the surrounding area is covered with flesh-eaters. You think Officer Brown was going to come here and save you? Once he took Isiah and Gillian, there wasn't any use for you. I bet they're being tortured right now as we speak for information about me. FUCK! We're at a dead end."

My stomach twisted up in knots, disabling me. I fell to the floor and Cree rushed to me.

"What's the matter with him? I'm going to wake up Latisha," Jacob told Cree. I vomited green blood and Cree panicked.

"What is happening? Is it hunger?" she asked.

Ba-boomp... Ba-boomp... Ba-boomp...

"Get back, Cree!" I said.

Latisha came into the kitchen. She pushed up my eyelids, examining my eyes.

"He's going through withdrawals. Are you an alcoholic or a drug user?" Latisha asked me. The pain was getting worse.

"He's ready to pass out! What do we do? We need him alive!" Jacob shrieked.

Cree untied her grandmother then pushed her on the floor next to me.

"What are you doing?" Latisha asked Cree.

"Feeding him," Cree said.

"That's your grandmother for crying out loud!" Latisha said to Cree.

"She once told me that sacrifices had to be made for a better future. Wolfsbane is my future so mind the business that pays you!" Cree said.

"I don't want you ha...hating me," I heaved. Nanny was screaming, trying to get away from Cree's grasp.

"I can't watch this," Latisha said.

"Eat her," Cree said.

If I had to describe how I emotionally felt, I was feeling like an animal. Cree throwing an old human at me, telling me to eat her, was a wake-up call as Jacob and Latisha looked at me in horror. The reality was that no matter what I did or how I felt, I was a monster. I was dying of starvation, but I couldn't eat Cree's grandmother because she was caught up in the moment. She loved her grandmother and would probably regret this later.

"What's going on?" Tray asked, coming into the kitchen.

"Help me," Nanny said to Tray.

"Why does Kyst look like that?" Tray asked.

"So he *is* the boy that killed that white cop. I knew I wasn't tripping," Latisha said.

"He did what needed to be done. Everyone, out of the kitchen! Jacob, tie Nanny back up and take her to the living room," Cree said. Nanny pulled on the doorknob of the back door to get away, but Jacob shoved her to the floor. Cree helped him put her grandmother back in the chair and tied her up.

"Why is an old woman being treated like this? This is cruel as fuck!" Tray said.

"She's responsible for a lot of missing children so stay out of it," Cree yelled at Tray.

"I didn't know, my bad," Tray said.

Tray, Latisha and Jacob left the kitchen. Cree smacked me to keep me from falling asleep. My clothes were drenched in sweat and my speech was slurring.

"What are you trying to accomplish? Are you trying to prove to us that you're still normal? You're pissing me off!" she said.

"You are tre...treating me li...like an animal. I don't need you throwing hum...an flesh at me like sc...raps from the table."

"Do you want me to let her go so that you can chase her?"

Nanny got loose from the chair; she wasn't tied tight enough. She grabbed a knife from the counter. It was too late by the time I warned Cree. Nanny stabbed her in the back. Cree fell into my body with her eyes wide-open.

"I'm sorry, baby, but I told you not to bring bad spirits into the house!" Nanny shouted at Cree. My body felt heavy as I tried to pull myself up. Latisha came into the kitchen. She shouted for help when Nanny stabbed Cree again. Tray beat Jacob to the kitchen. He twisted Nanny's arm to keep her from stabbing him. Latisha dragged Cree's body out of the kitchen and away from the commotion. Nanny tripped over me as Tray yanked the knife out of her hand. Nanny caterwauled when I bit a chunk out of her thin leg, splitting it in half. She reached out to Jacob for help; I pulled her back gnawing at her tough flesh to regain strength. Tray fainted and Jacob covered his mouth from puking. Minutes later, after eating Nanny's legs, throat and shoulders, I stood up, walking off-balance out of the kitchen. Latisha was in the hallway with Cree, holding her hand while she fought to breathe.

"She's not going to make it," Latisha sobbed.

SOUL Publications

I pulled Cree up and her body lazily draped over my arm. Her blood flooded the hallway. Her pulse was slowing down as she coughed up blood. I moved the hair out of her face, caressing her cheek. I waited for a light to flicker, indicating that she was only crossing over to the spirit world then coming back. She wiped the blood off my lips. "I'll be watching over you," she said. I cried like a baby, holding on to Cree. No words could explain how my non-beating heart shattered like glass.

"No, baby, no, don't say shit like that."

"I got to spend time with you in my final days. Don't let my death control your fate. Find Isiah and Gillian and get rid of the people responsible for the virus," she said. Cree was straining to get another word out but choked on her blood. I held on to her until she took her final breath.

"Why is God punishing me!" I shouted. Latisha rubbed my back while I cried over Cree. Nothing else came to mind at that moment, not even my family. I wished I had a chance to fully explore a relationship with Cree. She died with her eyes open. I closed her eyes so that she could peacefully rest then held on to her until the sun came up.

Two days later...

The past few days have been hard on me. I was cooped up in the bedroom me and Cree briefly shared. Her body was resting on the bed, wrapped in a blood-stained sheet. For two days, I didn't leave her side. I was waiting for her to wake up or feel her spirit's presence.

"It's okay if you blame me for your death. I should've eaten your bug-eyed grandmother when you told me to, but I couldn't because I was afraid that you were going to regret it and resent me."

Latisha knocked on the door before coming in.

"Jacob and Tray are finished digging the hole," she said. I kept putting off burying Cree.

"I'm not ready."

"We're never ready to bury a loved one but her body is going to start smelling," Latisha said. I picked up Cree's hand and her fingers were stiff.

"I'll bring her out soon."

Latisha held my hand in hers. "I'm here for you. We are all here for you, but she needs to be buried."

Latisha cut off a patch of Cree's hair then braided it. "Keep this with you," she said, wrapping the braid around my wrist like a bracelet.

"I'll be on the porch, waiting for you to bring her out," she said. Latisha left out of the bedroom and Tray came in, covered in mud.

"I never knew Cree was that beautiful. She was always getting smart whenever she saw me," Tray chuckled.

"Cree was always mean but underneath that layer was a heart of gold."

"I was wrong for how I reacted towards you and maybe this is the wrong time to talk about this, but I want to thank you for looking out for me. I couldn't had done it myself. You came at a time when I was most vulnerable and I'm here for you during your time of vulnerability, bro," he said. I slapped hands with him.

"Thanks, bro. At least me, you and Jacob are back together. After I bury her, I'm leaving for the safe zone. I'm sure Dr. Richmond has men there who know about Isiah. I'm going to torture their asses, too. I'm out for blood. The villain always gets the happy ending. I'm done being nice, bro. I don't want to be a hero."

"What do you want to be then, bro?" he nervously asked.

"A monster because good-hearted folks always end up like Cree."

"We are with you through whatever," Tray said.

I kissed Cree's lips one last time before pulling the sheet over her face. Tray held the bedroom door open for me as I carefully carried her out of the bedroom and out of the house. Jacob and Latisha were standing by a hole in the ground. Jacob made a cross for Cree with her favorite teddy bear on it. I jumped in the shallow grave to lay her to rest, next to her shot gun. After I climbed out, we had a moment of silence for her after we threw dirt on her body. Jacob broke the silence when he sobbed.

"I'm going to miss her, too," Jacob said.

"Me, too."

"I'm going to get our bags ready for the trip. They'll be by the door," Latisha said.

"I'll help her," Tray said, leaving.

Jacob shivered though it wasn't that chilly outside. The sun was shining bright and the temperature was around sixty degrees.

"You feel that? It got ice cold for a second," he said. I felt it, too, on the back of my neck.

"Yeah, there's a spirit here."

I hope it's you, Cree. I hope you stick with me through our journey.

"We have a long walk. It'll take three days to get to the safe zone."

"I hope my parents are there," Jacob said.

"Bet they will be. If not, I'll make sure you get to your vacation home safely."

Jacob left Cree's grave to prepare for the trip. I told her I loved her before walking away. A gust of wind touched my face.

I hope like hell that was a kiss, Cree.

I grabbed my backpack, leaving behind Cree's duffle bag. I planned on coming back to speak to her again. This wasn't the last of us. Before walking away from the cabin, I blew a kiss at Cree's grave.

Isiah

The Island

The next day...

I woke up with my head pounding like I consumed a fifth of Henny by myself. A drop of water falling from the ceiling rang in my ears.

"Arrghhh," I said, holding my head. I sat up adjusting my eyes because everything seemed big.

"Where the hell am I?"

I rolled over and landed on a cold concrete floor. The room was set up like a jail cell with monitors on the wall. A white old man came up on the screen and the static gave me a headache. Everything was coming back to me. I checked my leg because I remembered being shot but there weren't any signs of a bullet wound.

"You're finally up after being asleep for four days. You've healed well," he said.

"Where is Dr. Richmond?" I asked the man.

"He's in the lab, but I'm his father and whatever you need to tell him, you can tell me. Are you having any human cravings?" he asked.

"Where is Gillian? I hope she's alive!"

"She's in the room next to yours," he replied.

I threw myself against the steel door to break free, but it only dented a little, it didn't budge.

"Your strength isn't the same as your brother's, Isiah. He has two strands of the virus, you only have one until we inject you again," he said. I jumped on the bed to look out of the shoe box-sized window. From the looks of it, we were on an island.

"Yes, we're on an island, and there's no way for you to escape so you might as well listen," he said.

SOUL Publications

"Fuck you!"

"I'm here to help you and your family but first you need to calm down and listen carefully. We need you to cooperate and tell us where you think your brother might be. If you give us that, we'll send you off to a nice facility in Antarctica. We only want to run a few tests on him, we won't hurt him."

"Why do you need him if you're running tests on me? Leave my brother out of this!"

"We need him because he belongs to our lab. We can't have our experiments roaming around, especially someone special like him," he said.

I picked up a chair and swung it at the monitor, cracking the screen.

"Tomorrow morning, you'll be back in the lab but in the meantime, think about the lives your brother is ruining with his abilities. If you don't give us what we want, eventually you will suffer the consequences," he said.

The screen went blank; I was furious!

"Isiah!" a voice called out. I went to the vent on the bottom of the wall. I saw Gillian when I laid next to the vent. She cracked a weak smile; her face was bruised.

"Did they, you know... Did they use my sperm?"

"Not yet. They're waiting for you to have the second strand. I'm so scared but I'm very happy to see you. I thought you were dead," she sniffled.

"I'm happy to see you, too. Did anyone touch you?"

"Just back at the cabin. You have dark green eyes now, but your face is blemish-free. You look good, too bad it's because you're infected," she said.

"Only you would make a situation not as bad as it seems."

"You've got to smile to keep from frowning sometimes. If I do get pregnant, you'll have to take my virginity," she said. I chuckled listening to Gillian.

"Even if I do take your virginity, I want to work hard for it first"

"Food tray!" someone said through a monitor by my door. The compartment in the middle of the door opened and a tray of food was dropped inside my room, falling on the floor. It was a bloody brain. I saw a piece of paper sticking up in between.

"I'll be back," I told Gillian.

I picked up the brain, playing it off like I was eating it. I opened the letter with my back turned against the monitors. The letter said...

At midnight between shift changes, I'm going to help you escape; the same way I helped the prisoners at Rockstone. Let the girl know that there will be a building full of flesh-eaters tonight so she can be prepared. Also your father is alive but he's in a coma in the basement. Eat this letter! In three minutes, Dr. Richmond will be off break to monitor you.

Derrick

Is this the nigga, Derrick, that brought me here? Nanny's Derrick? And if so, why is he helping me now? I don't trust that nigga. What if it's a set-up? Got to be a set-up. There's no way in hell my father is alive, but then again, these scientists are clever. They can do just about anything. Shit, I'll just have to wait and see.

I went to the vent and Gillian was lying on her back from what I could see.

"At midnight, an outbreak will occur inside this building as a distraction so that we can escape."

"Who said that?" she asked.

"Someone gave me a letter."

"Do you trust it?" she asked.

"We don't have a choice. We have to wait until midnight to see."

"If it's true, you better protect me with your new abilities. I'm still a human and I won't last one minute in a building full of flesh-eaters," she said.

"Shorty I gotcha."

I'm going to leave this island, one way or another!

Cree

Is This the End?

*T*he people in the land of the forgotten were dancing around the campfire while I cried. I was dead and there was nothing I could do about it. I buried my face in my hands when Beth sat next to me.

"It's not the end, Cree. You'll go back but it'll take time," she said.

"I know we can't change fate; we wouldn't be here if we could."

"Look at me," she said.

I looked into her black eyes that constantly cried tears of blood.

"When there's a life inside of life, it blooms like a flower. Don't be unappreciative, the rest of them don't have a way to come back."

A little girl spirit came to me and sat on my lap. Since I was dead, they weren't just silhouettes. I was able to touch them.

"They are celebrating your life, you should join them," Beth said.

"I don't want to."

"Dance with me, Cree," the little girl said. She was about five years old.

"When I feel better."

"Okay," she said. She got off my lap and ran towards the dancing crowd.

"Do you know that you're infected?" Beth asked.

"Come again?"

"The baby that will grow inside your womb will bring you back to life." she said.

"What are you telling me, Beth?"

"The blood from your child is what will bring you back to life. You'll wake up craving flesh from a human."

"I'm pregnant?" I asked in disbelief.

"Yes," she said. She placed her hand on my stomach.

"Be careful when you go back. Wolfsbane is in a dark place because he thinks he lost you. He will not be the same man you shared intimacy with," she said. My happiness faded away in a snap of a finger.

"What do you mean?"

"There's another woman who will stop at nothing to fill in your shoes. A broken heart can lead into a forbidden passion," she said.

"I haven't been dead long. Why would he move on so quickly?"

Beth disappeared, leaving me sick to my stomach.

What did she mean by those things she said about Wolfsbane? And who could be the woman she was referring to? Does he love me? Why would he do something so stupid? There will be hell to pay if he betrays me and his unborn child!

To be continued....

SOUL Publications

*****Join Natavia's Paranormal Reads Facebook group for updates on her paranormal releases, book discussions and many more******

Coming Soon!!

Coming Soon!!